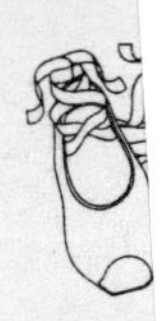

Everyone was onstage. We were about to rehearse Act I from the battle to the end. It included the scene where Dean had to kiss me.

The soldiers and mice had their big battle. Then it was time for our kiss. Dean was walking toward me. One step. Two. Three. Four. Even with my eyes closed I could feel everyone watching. At the last second I snatched my hand away.

"Aw, go ahead and kiss him," John Stein called.

I opened my eyes.

Dean looked furious. "Megan, we practiced this!"

"I bet you guys practice *all the time,*" one of the guys called.

"I'm telling you once and for all. I don't like Dean. I—I hate him!"

Dean's face turned bright red. He opened and closed his mouth, but no sound came out.

Why had I said that? It wasn't true. The other kids started to leave. They were whispering about what had happened. I had ruined rehearsal. And I was going to ruin the whole ballet.

Also available in this series

4 Megan's Nutcracker Prince

EMILY COSTELLO

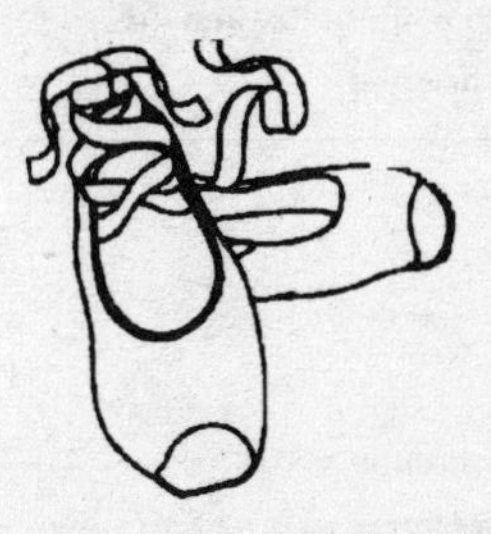

ILLUSTRATED BY MARCY RAMSEY

This book is a work of fiction. Names, characters, places, and incidents are products of the author's imagination or are used fictitiously. Any resemblance to actual events or locales or persons, living or dead, is entirely coincidental.

First published in the USA 1994
by HarperPaperbacks, a division of HarperCollins Publishers

First published in Great Britain 1997
by Mammoth, an imprint of Reed International Books Ltd
Michelin House, 81 Fulham Road, London SW3 6RB
and Auckland and Melbourne

Illustrations by Marcy Ramsey
Cover illustration by David Browne

ISBN 0 7497 2710 1

10 9 8 7 6 5 4 3 2 1

A CIP catalogue record for this title
is available from the British Library

Printed Great Britain
by Cox & Wyman Ltd, Reading, Berkshire

This book is for Françoise Bui, with thanks for her encouragement and graceful criticism.

One

An Important Class

"What time is it?" I gasped.

"It's three twenty-one," my best friend, Jillian Kormach, answered.

"The most important ballet class of the year starts in nine minutes," Becky Hill said. "We'll be late if we don't hurry." She started to run.

It was the Tuesday before Thanksgiving. Jillian, Becky, and I raced down Main Street. When we got to Madame Trikilnova's Classical Ballet School, we dashed up the steps and rushed into the dressing room.

Our friends were already there, in their ballet clothes. Nikki Norg, Katie Ruiz, and Risa Cumberland were dressed in pink leotards, pink tights, and pink ballet slippers. All of the intermediate dancers at our school wear pink to class.

My friends and I call ourselves Pat's Pinks. Pat is our teacher. Our class meets on Tuesday and Thursday afternoons.

"How come you're so late?" Nikki greeted us.

"We didn't think you'd get here on time," Risa added.

"Did you forget that Madame Trikilnova is coming to class today?" Katie asked.

Becky kicked off her shoes. "We didn't forget!"

"We got here as fast as we could," Jillian added.

Madame Trikilnova owns our ballet school. I always get nervous when she comes to our class. But that day I was extra nervous. Madame Trikilnova was coming for an important reason. She was going to watch us dance, and decide who would make the best Clara in *The Nutcracker*.

The Nutcracker is a ballet that takes place on Christmas Eve. It's about a girl named Clara who has a nutcracker doll that turns into a real prince.

At our school Clara is always played by a ten-year-old girl. My friends and I all wanted to be Clara. So did the rest of the girls in our ballet class.

"Ms. Rosen made us stay after school," I told my friends. Becky, Jillian, and I are all in Ms. Rosen's fourth-grade class at Glory Elementary.

"How come?" Nikki asked.

"Becky was whispering," Jillian said. She wiggled out of her jeans. "She got all three of us in trouble."

"That's not fair," Becky said. "You were whispering, too."

"We were *all* whispering," I said.

"About what?" Risa asked.

"About being Clara," Becky said, tucking a piece of copper-colored hair behind her ear and letting out a dreamy sigh. "About standing onstage in the spotlight while everyone claps. About getting flowers on opening night."

"You'd better get your head out of the clouds," Katie told Becky. "You don't have much time to get ready." Katie always drags us back to earth when we get starry-eyed.

Becky stuck her tongue out at Katie.

"Katie and I got in trouble today, too," Risa reported. "I couldn't stop talking about being Clara, either." Risa and Katie go to the same private school. Nikki goes to my school, but she's a grade ahead of the rest of us.

"Risa's even wearing a good-luck ribbon," Katie told us.

Risa is African-American. She always wears her hair in a ponytail on top of her head. She had on a pink-and-white polka-dotted ribbon.

Wearing something special for luck is not Katie's style. She had on her oldest leotard, and tights with runs in them. Katie's brown hair was up in a messy bun.

I pulled my leotard and tights out of my bag.

"Megan," Katie said to me. "Your hands are shaking!"

I'm used to having butterflies in my stomach before ballet class. Ballet is a struggle for me. I'm always worried about making mistakes. But I was way beyond butterflies that afternoon. My stomach felt like eagles were flapping around inside.

"If you guys are this nervous today, what are you going to be like on Saturday?" Nikki asked.

"Just as nervous," Becky said.

The official *Nutcracker* tryouts were on Saturday, four days away. That's when Madame Trikilnova would pass out all of the kids' roles.

Of course, there were also adult roles in the ballet.

Three dancers were coming all the way from Russia to dance the biggest ones. The smaller ones would be performed by the most advanced kids in our school.

I was excited because one of the Russian dancers was going to stay with my family. Another one was staying with Jillian. And the last one was staying with Charlotte Stype, the snobbiest girl in our ballet class.

"Is Dean excited?" Katie asked as I yanked up my tights.

"How would I know?" I asked.

The other girls glanced at me. They were trying not to laugh.

Dean Stellar is in my class at regular school and my class at ballet school. He's got curly light-brown hair and blue eyes. Sometimes Dean and I have nice talks. But most of the time, he hits me, pinches me, and teases me. Somehow my friends have gotten the crazy idea that Dean likes me. They're always acting like he's my boyfriend or something. I hate it.

"Dean was throwing spitballs at Megan all through geography," Jillian reported.

"If you ask me, that proves it," Risa said.

I put my arms into the sleeves of my leotard. "Right. It proves that geography is boring."

"It proves that Dean likes you," Jillian said.

"I've told you guys a million times," I said. "Dean doesn't like me. And I don't like him."

"Sure, Megan," Katie said.

"I believe you," Jillian added. *I believe you* is what Jillian says when she *doesn't* believe you. That is one habit of hers that really bugs me.

"Do you want me to help you with your hair?" Nikki asked.

"Yes," I said. Buns are a must for ballet class. It takes me forever to get my long hair to stay up in one.

Nikki is good at making buns because she used to have super-long hair. She got it all cut off last summer. Madame Trikilnova was angry when she first saw Nikki's haircut. She thinks ballerinas have to have long hair. Still, Nikki refuses to grow it out. That's because she looks great with short hair.

While Nikki brushed my hair, I put on my ballet slippers.

My left slipper has an "L" written on it. The "L" is big enough so that I can see it clearly when I'm dancing. But it's small enough so that people don't ask me about it.

See, during class, Pat tells us stuff like, "start with your left foot." I have a hard time remembering which foot is which. By the time I figure it out, the class is usually halfway through the exercise we're doing. Jillian thought of the "L." It makes ballet much easier.

"If you don't get to be Clara, what part is your second choice?" Becky asked all of us.

"I want to be a party guest," I said right away.

"Party guest," Jillian agreed.

The others nodded.

When *The Nutcracker* opens, it's Christmas Eve. Clara's family is having a big party. Lots of the party guests are kids. Pat says it's a fun scene to be in.

Nikki, Katie, and I had been in *The Nutcracker* the year before. We were angels. It was so much fun! Our part was easy. And since we were all together, I wasn't nervous. This time last year Jillian was still living in New York. She had been an angel in a production of *The Nutcracker* there. This was the first year Becky and Risa had tried out for the ballet.

"Finished!" Nikki announced.

"Thanks," I said.

"Yikes!" Becky yelled. "It's three thirty. Let's go!"

We rushed up the stairs. The eagles in my stomach started to do somersaults.

"I'm scared," Becky whispered.

"Don't be silly," I said. "You're going to be great."

"Thanks," Becky said. She has a perfect dancer's body—tall, slim, and strong. Becky is one of the best dancers in our class. She takes dance seriously. She wants to be a ballerina when she grows up.

We hurried down the second-floor hallway. But when we got to the studio, I hesitated. I was afraid to go in.

"Come on," Jillian said. She grabbed my hand and pulled me after her. Jillian is beautiful—her skin is the color of chocolate milk, and her eyes are huge. Plus, she used to live in New York City. Both those things make her brave.

Madame Trikilnova was already in the studio. She was standing near the piano, chatting with Al, our piano player.

The rest of the class was there, too. You already know about Dean. The others are Philip Stellar (Dean's twin brother), John Stein, Charlotte Stype, Lynn Frazier, and Kim Woyczek.

Madame Trikilnova was wearing her usual: a black leotard and a long, flowing black skirt. Her blond hair was tucked into a neat bun at the back of her neck. Al looked funny standing next to Madame Trikilnova. He's every bit as messy as she is tidy. He has pale skin and a messy mop of brown hair. Al's a little strange. He likes to stick his tongue out at people. Sometimes Al and I talk about music. I love music, and he knows a lot about it.

"Hello, Miss Isozaki," Madame Trikilnova said to me.

"Hello," I said.

I love the way Madame Trikilnova calls us by our last names. It sounds so grand. Also, I think my name is beautiful. It says a lot about me. Megan is an Irish name. Isozaki is a Japanese one. Just like my name, I'm fifty percent Irish (that's my mother's side) and fifty percent Japanese (that's my father's side).

I turned ten last July. My first year in double digits! That makes me feel grown up. Too bad I look about seven. I'm really skinny. If I cut off my hair like Nikki did, I'd probably only weigh about half as much as I do now. But I'll never cut my hair. It's my favorite thing about myself. It's brownish black, and it comes down almost to my waist.

My friends and I found places at the barre. I didn't want to, but I forced myself to take the front spot. Usually—that is, when Madame Trikilnova *isn't* in our class—we stand wherever we want. I like to hide in the back. But Madame Trikilnova says short people like me belong in front.

Pat came in. She nodded to Madame Trikilnova and then turned to face us. Pat seemed startled to see me in front. She winked at me. I smiled back and started to feel better.

Pat has shiny black hair, pale skin, and freckles. She's beautiful and the nicest ballet teacher in the world.

"Let's get started," Pat called. "We'll begin with *demi-pliés*. Down in two counts, up in two counts. Don't rush them."

Demi-plié is French for half knee-bend. (Most words for ballet steps are in French. That's because the first ballet school in the whole world was in France.)

Al started to play a slow song.

We put our left hands on the barre and eased into a *demi-plié.* (A barre is a wooden handrail that runs around the walls of a ballet studio. You hold on to it while you do exercises to warm up your muscles.)

I like ballet, but it's hard for me. I have to practice the steps we do in class at home every day. Otherwise, I forget them. That's why I like the barre exercises better than the other parts of ballet class. They're pretty much the same from class to class. I don't have to worry about new steps.

The part of class that comes next, center work, is okay, too. During center work we repeat many of the barre exercises, but without holding on to the barre. I know what to expect.

Traveling steps and combinations, the last part of ballet class, are the worst, if you ask me.

Combinations are a bunch of steps put into a mini-dance. For some reason, the steps always get scrambled in my brain. I mess them up a lot.

We did four *demi-pliés*. Then Pat called, "*Relevé* and turn." We all rose up on the balls of our feet and turned until we were facing the other direction.

Out of the corner of my eye I saw Madame Trikilnova walk over to Becky. She watched her dance while we did four more *demi-pliés*. We turned to face front again.

"Okay," Pat called. "Let's move on to *grand pliés*. Four counts down, four counts up." A *grand plié* is a deep knee-bend.

As we started *grand pliés,* Madame Trikilnova went to stand next to Jillian. I groaned softly. What if Madame Trikilnova came and stood next to *me*? I felt like running away.

We finished our *grand pliés*.

"Okay," Pat called. "Let's put some *grand pliés* and *relevés* together. I want you to *plié* on one and two. Take the next four counts to *relevé* all the way up onto the balls of your feet. With the last two counts come back to center. Ready, and one—"

Madame Trikilnova walked over and stood next to me.

I tried to pretend she wasn't there. It shouldn't have been hard. I've had a lot of practice pretending my older brother, Conrad, doesn't exist. Sometimes, when I'm ignoring him (or trying to), he burps in my ear.

Madame Trikilnova didn't burp. But she was still hard to ignore. I was relieved when she whispered, "Nice work," and moved on.

After we finished our barre exercises, Pat told us we were going to skip center work. "I want to go straight to a combination," she announced. Then she showed us what to do.

We were supposed to *plié* and then *relevé*. Next came a *pas de bourrée* (that's a kind of traveling step) and then a *pirouette* (that's a turn).

None of my friends looked alarmed. Most of them like combinations. I wasn't happy. I didn't want to spend the rest of the class doing combinations.

Becky, Charlotte, and Dean were in the first group.

I danced in the last one with Philip and Kim. I forgot a step about halfway through, but I just looked over to see what Kim was doing. I got through the combination without making any major mistakes.

"Miss Hill," Madame Trikilnova said after my group had finished. "Would you please do that for me again?"

"By myself?" Becky asked.

Madame Trikilnova nodded.

Becky grinned. She was happy to be singled out. Al began to play, and Becky danced. When she finished, Madame Trikilnova and Pat whispered to each other.

"Good job," I told Becky. "You'd make a great Clara."

"Thanks!" Becky grinned. "I really want the part."

"Mr. Stellar," Madame Trikilnova said, nodding at Dean. "Let's see what you can do."

Dean stepped forward. He didn't look nervous at all. My heart started to race. Dean might not have been nervous, but I was nervous for him.

Here's the scoop: I actually do like Dean, but I don't want my friends to know. My heart gets fluttery when I see him. I pretend it's not happening because, no matter what my friends say, there's *no way* Dean would like me. Why would he? I'm not beautiful like Jillian. Or smart like Katie. Or a terrific dancer like Becky. My friends are all special in some way. Nikki is funny. Risa has style. But me? The most unusual thing about me is that I'm a ten-year-old who looks like a first-grader.

"Thank you," Madame Trikilnova told Dean. "Miss Stype, would you please dance now?"

Charlotte stepped forward.

Jillian made a face.

None of my friends like Charlotte. (Not even Becky, who usually likes everyone.) Charlotte is tall, blond, and a good dancer. She acts like she's a princess.

"Miss Isozaki," Madame Trikilnova said. "Will you please do the combination?"

Me? Why? It didn't make sense. Becky, Dean, and Charlotte were the best dancers in our class. I could understand why Madame Trikilnova had singled them out. But me?

Katie pushed me forward.

Al began to play. But I was so surprised and nervous, I couldn't remember how the combination began. I didn't move. Al stopped playing.

Charlotte giggled.

"That's okay," Pat told me. "You can start again. Begin with a *plié*."

I nodded.

Al started to play.

Madame Trikilnova was watching me closely. I couldn't guess what she was thinking.

I did a *plié,* and the rest of the combination came to me in a rush. I did the steps without thinking about them. All I was thinking about was how to get away from Madame Trikilnova's eyes.

When I finished, Pat and Madame Trikilnova whispered some more. Then Madame Trikilnova said good-bye and slipped out the studio door.

"Okay," Pat told us. "That's all we have time for today. You guys did a good job. I'm sure Madame Trikilnova was impressed."

Everyone started clapping. It's a tradition to clap for your teacher and piano player after a ballet

class. Pat and Al clap for us, too. Pat says we work just as hard as they do.

"I'm so glad that's over," I said.

"You did a good job," Becky told me.

I laughed. "You did much better. I'm sure you'll get to be Clara."

Becky grinned. "I hope so!"

"One of you guys will get it," Risa said. "You both danced well."

"It doesn't matter how well they danced!" Charlotte said. She had snuck up behind us. "Because *I'm* going to be Clara in *The Nutcracker*."

"You don't know that!" Katie exploded. "It could be Becky . . . it could be any of us."

"Sure," Charlotte said. "Maybe it will be Megan." Charlotte thought that was really funny. She cracked up. She was still laughing as she left the studio.

My face felt hot. I clenched my fists.

"I can't believe Charlotte said that," Risa said.

"Don't listen to her," Jillian told me. "You're a good dancer. You just got a little nervous today."

"I don't care who gets to be Clara," Becky said, "just as long as it isn't Charlotte."

Two

Bad Grades

"How did you do?" Becky whispered to me the next afternoon at school.

"Um—not too bad," I replied.

We had just gotten our report cards. Ms. Rosen passed them out right before the final bell.

"I got an *A* in spelling," Jillian announced.

"Lucky," Becky said. "I only got a *B*-plus."

Jillian smiled. "Luck had nothing to do with it. I worked hard in spelling."

I had worked hard in spelling, too. But I had gotten a *D*. The rest of my grades were *C*s and *C*-minuses. My grades get worse every year.

The bell rang. Jillian, Becky, and I jumped up and rushed toward the door. We always walk part of the way home together.

"Megan," Ms. Rosen called. "May I speak to you for a minute?"

"Sure," I said. My stomach did a quick flip-flop. What did Ms. Rosen want?

"We'll wait for you outside," Jillian said.

Becky nodded.

"Okay," I agreed.

Ms. Rosen is a nice but no-nonsense teacher. On the first day of school she told us she had eyes in the back of her head. Maybe she really does. She always knows when someone is fooling around.

"Please give this to your parents," Ms. Rosen said. She handed me an envelope. "It says that I want them to come in for a parent-teacher conference."

"Okay," I said, taking the envelope.

I walked outside feeling awful. Becky and Jillian were sitting in the grass in front of the school.

"What did Blue Hair want?" Jillian asked. She calls Ms. Rosen that because her hair is a sort of silvery blue.

I shrugged. "She wants my parents to come in to see her."

"Why?" Becky asked.

"She didn't really say," I replied. It wasn't a lie. I knew Ms. Rosen wanted my parents to come in because of my grades. But she hadn't come straight out and said it.

"Come on," I said. "I'm sick of school. Let's go."

Becky, Jillian, and I headed for home, talking about our plans for Thanksgiving.

I didn't want my friends to know about my

report card. Jillian and Becky are both smart. They're in the top reading group in Ms. Rosen's class, the Jaguars. The other reading groups are the Giraffes, Zebras, Bears, Wolves, and Deer. I'm not in any of them. I'm in a reading group all by myself. It doesn't have a name.

When I got home, I went straight to my room. My parents weren't home. Neither was Conrad.

My room is my favorite place in our house. It's on the first floor, just off the kitchen. Mom says it used to be a maid's room. It's tiny. My room has all the usual stuff: books, posters, and stuffed animals. It also has several exceptional things: a turntable for records, two speakers, and a pair of headphones. My uncle Mark gave me his old stereo system last year. He bought a new one that has a CD player.

Uncle Mark also gave me all of his old records—jazz, rock, and classical stuff. It took me months to listen to all the records for the first time.

I put on an old Beatles album and sat down at my desk. I studied my report card. It was awful. I thought about starting my homework, but that seemed silly. It was Wednesday of Thanksgiving weekend. I didn't have school for four days. I got up and pushed in my desk chair. I stood in second position in front of my full-length mirror. I tried to remember the combination we had learned in ballet the day before. It started with a *plié,* that much I remembered. But what came next? A *relevé*? I was still trying to remember when I heard the front door open.

"Hi, honey." Mom poked her head into my room. "We went to the grocery store, and there's lots to unpack. Come out and help."

Mom has red hair that's just as long as mine. She's skinny. She wears blue jeans that hang off her hips. Mom is a *potter*. A potter is someone who makes things out of clay.

When I came into the kitchen, the table and counters were covered with brown bags.

My father was unpacking the food. I call him O-tosan, which is Japanese for "father." He has straight black hair, black eyes, and dark skin. O-tosan is a potter, too. He also plays the flute. He was going to be in the orchestra for *The Nutcracker*.

"What is all this stuff?" I asked.

O-tosan wiggled his eyebrows at me. "We bought a Thanksgiving feast. A turkey, cranberries, potatoes, sweet potatoes, stuffing, and apples for a pie. I'm going to cook all day tomorrow."

"It will be nice to have a break from work," Mom said.

Mom and O-tosan have a studio and shop outside of Glory. They make pottery in the studio and sell it in the shop.

When potters make something, they say they are "throwing" a pot or a mug or whatever. I could tell Mom had been throwing that day, because she was covered with clay. She even had some in her hair. Mom says pottery is a messy business.

"I have something to tell you guys," I announced.

"Can it wait until after I shower?" Mom asked. "I think I got clay in my *ears* today. The grocer wasn't too happy to see me coming."

"It's just that I got my report card," I said. "I'll show it to you later."

O-tosan stopped unpacking the groceries.

"I'd like to see that right away," Mom said.

"What about your shower?" I asked.

"It can wait," Mom decided.

I had no choice but to go into my room, get my report card and the letter from Ms. Rosen, and give them to my parents. Mom and O-tosan studied my report card without speaking for a long time. Then they read the letter. I couldn't tell what they were thinking, but I knew they weren't surprised. I never do well in school.

Finally, O-tosan sighed. "You're going to have to work harder, Megan."

Tears came to my eyes. "I'm already working *very* hard." It was true. That whole year, I had been trying especially hard. I always paid attention whenever Ms. Rosen was talking.

"I know you're trying," Mom said. "But, well—it seems like you have to try harder. Maybe you're rushing through your work."

"I'm not rushing!" I yelled. "It takes me forever to do my homework."

Mom didn't argue with that. She knew it was true.

"None of your teachers has ever requested a conference before," O-tosan pointed out. "Have you been bad?"

"No," I said, looking down at the floor.

I'm always good and I always do my best at school. My best just isn't good enough. Why didn't my parents understand that?

The back door banged open. Conrad stomped in. "I'm dropping out of school!" he announced. "My English teacher says I don't belong in the seventh grade."

"Calm down," Mom told Conrad.

"Did you get your report card today?" O-tosan asked.

Conrad held it out.

I went back into my room. Even with the door closed, I could hear my parents arguing with Conrad. His grades must have been as bad as mine. I flopped down on my bed and buried my face in my pillow. The next day was Thanksgiving. Ha! What did I have to be thankful for?

Three

Charlotte Shows Off

Nutcracker tryouts were on the Saturday after Thanksgiving, at ten o'clock.

"Children!" Madame Trikilnova was yelling as I walked into the theater. "Sit with your classes! Parents, please wait in the lobby!"

I hurried to join my class. Everyone except for Charlotte, Lynn, and the twins was already there.

"Am I late?" I asked after I said hello to my friends.

Katie shook her head. "Tryouts don't start for fifteen minutes."

I looked around. "Everyone's early."

Al was at the piano. He was eating a lollipop and studying some music.

Pat was talking to another teacher.

"People are early because they're nervous," Nikki said. "I woke up at six o'clock this morning."

"I got nervous last night," Risa said with a yawn.

"I couldn't get to sleep until midnight."

I sat down. My tights and leotard were on under my clothes. I pulled off my jeans and sweatshirt, and put them on the seat next to me. I changed into my ballet slippers.

"Are you nervous?" Jillian asked me.

I nodded. "O-tosan made me breakfast, but I couldn't eat a bite."

"Maybe you're still full from Thanksgiving," Risa said.

I shook my head. "I have butterflies."

"I know what you mean." Becky put a hand on her stomach. "Mom made me eat an egg. Ugh."

"My mom made pancakes with strawberries and bananas," Katie announced. "I had seconds." Katie loves to eat.

"Pancakes?" I groaned. "I don't want to hear about it!"

"There's no reason to be nervous," Katie said. "We're just going to dance for teachers from our school. It's not much different from going to class."

Risa looked at Katie like she was crazy. "This is just like class?" She motioned out into the theater. Kids and parents were swarming all over. Practically the entire ballet school was there.

Katie giggled. "Like class with a really big audience."

Becky took a shaky breath. "Can we please talk about something else?"

I smiled. "I love this place."

Most of the year, movies are shown at the Glory theater. But a long time ago, before movies were so popular, it was used for live performances. Traveling singers, actors, and musicians used to perform in the theater. It has a stage, a pit for musicians, curtains, wings, and everything. Every December, the owner takes down the movie screen and allows Madame Trikilnova to use the theater for *The Nutcracker*.

"My grandma and grandpa used to come here on dates," Jillian told us. Her grandparents have lived in Glory all their lives.

I plan to live in Glory my whole life, too. It's so small, practically everyone knows everyone else. I like that. Also, it's green and quiet and peaceful.

"I think I'm going to throw up," Becky announced.

I groaned. "We were *trying* to change the subject."

"It wasn't working," Becky said, hugging her stomach.

Pat came over to us. "How are you guys feeling?"

"Awful," Becky told her.

"Don't worry," Pat said. "The tryouts are going to be easy. You'll do great."

Lynn and Charlotte came down the aisle. Charlotte was wearing a brand-new pair of ballet slippers. Her hair was held back by a sparkling headband. She didn't look at all nervous.

"Okay, everybody, it's ten o'clock," Madame Trikilnova called. "We're going to start."

I looked around the theater. "Where are Dean and Philip?"

"I don't think they're here yet," Jillian told me.

"I hope Dean doesn't miss the tryout," I said.

"Let's have all the Blues onstage," Madame Trikilnova called. The Blues are the beginning dancers. They're called Blues because they wear blue leotards to class.

Once all Blues were onstage, Madame Trikilnova asked them to run around in a big circle. She stood in the center of the circle—watching and frowning.

"Did I miss it?" a breathless voice asked in my ear.

I turned around. I was face-to-face with Dean. My heart started to pound. "No, you're just in time."

A few seconds later Madame Trikilnova called our group. Remember those eagles? They were back in my stomach.

"Hey, Megan," Dean said. "Don't mess up."

"Yeah," I said. "Good luck."

Jillian and I were two of the first people onstage. "What do you think she's going to make us do?" I whispered while we waited for everyone else.

"Something hard," Jillian said.

I tried to swallow, but my throat was too dry.

"Line up!" Madame Trikilnova called. "I want to

see each of you do an *emboité*. One at a time, please."

Jillian and I traded looks. An *emboité*? That was easy!

An *emboité* is a jump. This is how you do it:

Start in fifth position with your right foot back. *Demi-plié* and spring into the air. Bring your right foot forward with your knee slightly bent. Land on your left foot with your right foot just in front of your left ankle. It should be a small, graceful step.

The kids from my class and the kids from Intermediate II formed a line. (Intermediate II is a Pink class that's harder than mine. Pat teaches it. The Intermediate II girls are mostly eleven- and twelve-year-olds.)

Charlotte was the first kid from my class to go. She must have been sad we didn't get to do something flashy, because she did a huge *emboité*. She jumped way up and threw her leg high into the air.

Katie rolled her eyes at me. Charlotte was such a show-off! I hoped Madame Trikilnova wasn't impressed.

The rest of us did our *emboités*. Dean did a normal-sized one. So did I. So did my friends. We didn't want to show off like Charlotte.

"Miss Stype," Madame Trikilnova said. "May I see another *emboité*, please?"

Charlotte looked so smug. She stepped forward, took three running steps in time with the music, and jumped. But this time Charlotte tried to jump too high. When she came down, she wobbled and fell.

"Let me do it again," Charlotte said, scrambling to her feet. "I only fell because I have new slippers."

"That's okay," Madame Trikilnova said. "I don't need to see another."

"That's what you get for showing off," Katie whispered.

"Miss Isozaki?" Madame Trikilnova said.

My head snapped up. "Yes?"

"May I see another *emboité,* please?"

"Don't think about it," Jillian said. "Just do it."

I stepped forward, took my running steps, and jumped. Then I ran back to my friends. They were all smiling.

"Good job," Jillian whispered.

"Miss Hill?" Madame Trikilnova called.

Becky did a beautiful *emboité*. Madame Trikilnova also called on Katie and Jillian. They were good, too.

"Okay, Pinks," Madame Trikilnova said then. "You're finished for now. Have a seat. But don't leave the theater."

Nikki skipped off the stage.

"Why are you happy?" Risa asked. "Madame Trikilnova didn't call on either of us. We're definitely not going to be Clara."

Nikki smiled a wicked smile. "I'm happy because Charlotte messed up!"

Four

A Star Is Born

"May I have the Blacks onstage!" Madame Trikil-nova hollered. The Blacks are the advanced dancers. They wear black leotards to class.

My friends and I were sitting in the theater, watching the rest of the tryouts. Dean had taken the seat behind us.

"I feel much better now," Becky announced.

"So do I," I agreed. "Except I'm hungry."

"Me too," Becky said.

"I thought you guys were going to throw up," Katie said.

Becky shrugged. "That was *before* we tried out."

"How do you think we did?" I asked.

Dean leaned forward. "You did well," he told me. "Your *emboité* was great."

"So was yours," I said.

Dean grinned.

My face felt hot. I'm sure my friends would have

started teasing me if Mrs. Kim, the Blues' teacher, hadn't come along. "Let's give the Blacks some quiet," she said.

I settled into my seat and watched the action on-stage.

Madame Trikilnova asked the older kids to do a lot of stuff: a series of flashy *pirouettes* (that means turns), *arabesques* (that's when you stand on one leg and extend the other out to the back), and lots of jumps.

"Can I have everyone onstage, please?" Madame Trikilnova called after she finished with the big kids.

We jumped up and ran up to the stage. Now that the trying-out part was over, I was having fun. We gathered around Madame Trikilnova. The other teachers were standing behind her. Pat winked at me.

"As most of you know, I'm going to give out parts in a minute," Madame Trikilnova started. "But first, I want to say that you all did well today."

Jillian grinned at me.

"However," Madame Trikilnova went on, "most of you will not get the part you want."

Jillian's grin faded.

"Every year, I give out roles for *The Nutcracker,*" Madame Trikilnova said. "And every year, children complain about my decisions. I've had kids cry and shout and call me names. But no one has ever convinced me to change my mind."

I started to chew on my fingernail.

Katie pulled my hand out of my mouth. "Relax," she whispered.

"If you wonder why you didn't get a certain part, remember there's more to being a good dancer than having talent." Madame Trikilnova looked right at me. "A good dancer must also follow instructions, arrive on time for rehearsals, and respect everyone else onstage."

I felt worse than I did before the tryouts. Forget about being Clara. I was worried about getting *any* part.

Madame Trikilnova looked down at her clipboard. She chose a Blue named Tad to be Fritz, Clara's little brother. Tad was happy. Little boys like being Fritz because he is naughty. He breaks Clara's nutcracker doll. That part of the ballet is pretty true to life, if you ask me. Conrad is always breaking my stuff.

Madame Trikilnova wrote something down. "Now for the party guests."

"Please let her pick me," I whispered.

Jillian showed me her hands. She had her fingers crossed.

"Boys first," Madame Trikilnova said. "Mr. Stein, Mr. Ryan, Mr. Brown, and Mr. Dalone." John Stein was in my class, of course. The other three boys were in the Intermediate II class.

"We don't have enough boys to be party guests," Madame Trikilnova added. "So some girls are going to have to take boys' parts." She pointed at Kim and Nikki. "Miss Woyczek and Miss Norg, you will be male party guests."

Nikki groaned.

"Now for the girls," Madame Trikilnova said.

I crossed my fingers, too. First Madame Trikilnova chose two girls from the Intermediate II class. Then she picked Risa, Katie, and Jillian. The three of them jumped up and down, and hugged each other.

"Who doesn't have a part yet?" Jillian whispered when she had calmed down.

"Lynn, Charlotte, Becky, and me," I replied.

"That means one of you will be Clara," Risa said.

"And one of us will be a party guest," I said.

"But the other two will get yucky parts," Becky added.

Madame Trikilnova waited for quiet before she went on. "Okay, our last party guest will be—"

"Please pick me," I whispered.

"Miss Hill," Madame Trikilnova said.

Becky looked crushed. She had really wanted to be Clara.

I did my best to hide how let down I was. I was sure I was going to get a yucky part.

Charlotte looked thrilled. She must have been certain she would be Clara. Lynn gave her a quick hug.

"Mr. Stellar, you will be the prince," Madame Trikilnova told Dean.

"Yes!" Dean exclaimed.

A few people patted Dean on the back. I smiled at him. Nobody was surprised Dean had been chosen.

I wasn't looking forward to the next announcement. I knew exactly what was going to happen. Madame Trikilnova would pick Charlotte to be Clara. And then Charlotte would gloat, gloat, gloat.

"Our Clara will be Miss Isozaki," Madame Trikilnova said.

Me!

Jillian let out a screech. She threw her arms around me.

"Way to go," Becky said.

Dean was grinning. "All right, Megan!"

Everyone—except for Charlotte—came over to congratulate me. My friends were jumping around and smiling and laughing. I didn't move or talk or even *breathe*. I had gotten the best part in the whole ballet! Never in my life had I been more surprised.

"Are you mad at me?" I whispered to Becky.

"No way," Becky said. "I'm happy for you."

"Let me have your attention," Madame Trikilnova finally called.

Things quieted down.

"Who's Megan's understudy?" Charlotte demanded.

"Miss Hill," Madame Trikilnova said.

My friends started to jump up and down again. This time, I joined in.

Charlotte looked furious. "Well, who will be Becky's understudy?"

"Understudies don't have understudies," Madame Trikilnova said. She sounded amused.

"Why not?" Charlotte insisted. "Becky and Megan could both get sick."

"Fine," Madame Trikilnova said. "Miss Stype, you can be Miss Hill's understudy."

"Charlotte is crazy," I said.

Becky nodded. "If you're sick, I'm definitely going to be here."

"This is perfect," Katie whispered, wiggling her eyebrows. "Dean is going to be your Nutcracker Prince—just like he's your prince in real life."

"Katie," I said in a warning tone.

Madame Trikilnova went on giving out parts. Most of my friends were going to be soldiers. (Almost everyone in the ballet has two parts.) Lynn and Charlotte would be mice.

People kept coming up to congratulate me on getting Clara. I was starting to feel like a famous ballerina.

"Happy?" Jillian asked.

I did a *pirouette*. "Absolutely." This was going to be fun!

Five

Worrywarts

Nutcracker tryouts were over. My friends and I were hanging around in front of the theater. I was waiting for my father to pick me up.

"I'm so happy for you," Jillian said.

"Thanks," I said.

"Your parents are going to be proud," Becky said.

I grinned. Becky was right. Now that I was Clara, maybe my parents would even forget about my terrible grades.

O-tosan pulled up in front of the theater. He and Conrad had come from the shop to pick me up.

"Bye," my friends yelled.

I waved to them and climbed into the backseat. "Hi," I said to Conrad and O-tosan.

"Hi." O-tosan pulled away from the curb.

Conrad turned around in his seat. "How was your tryout?"

"You'll never believe it," I said. "I'm going to be Clara!"

"Isn't that the biggest part?" O-tosan asked.

"It's the biggest part for a kid," I said.

"Cool," Conrad said. He held out his hand, and I slapped it. "My little sister is going to be a star."

I grinned. I suddenly understood why famous people are called stars. I was so happy, I felt as if I were giving off light. But then I saw O-tosan's reflection in the rearview mirror. He didn't look proud. He looked worried.

"I think it's terrific Madame Trikilnova chose you for the part," O-tosan said. He was speaking slowly. I could hear the "but" in his voice.

My mouth went dry. "What's wrong?"

"How much do you have to rehearse?" O-tosan asked.

"I forgot to ask," I said. "Why?"

"I was thinking about your grades," O-tosan said. "I don't want *The Nutcracker* to take too much time away from your studies."

"It won't," I said. "I have plenty of time to rehearse and do my homework."

"Yeah," Conrad said. "She just won't watch as much TV."

"I want to talk to your mom about this," O-tosan told me.

"Everyone wanted this part!" I said. "I can't turn it down."

"I'll discuss it with your mother," O-tosan repeated.

I pouted for the rest of the ride. As soon as O-tosan parked the car outside the shop, I climbed out and ran inside. I wanted to tell Mom my good news before O-tosan convinced her it was bad news.

My parents' store is small but tidy. It has big windows. Mugs, bowls, and platters are arranged on low tables. My parents have a stereo in the shop. Soothing music is always playing.

When I walked in, Mom was wrapping up a huge platter for a woman who was dressed all in beige. Another woman, with bushy red hair, was examining the mugs.

December is a busy month in my parents' shop. Everyone is doing their Christmas shopping. Conrad and I help out as much as we can. We wait on people and help Mom and O-tosan in the studio. I'm good at making handles for mugs, and wedging clay. That's what potters call squashing the air bubbles out.

"Mom!" I yelled. "Guess what? I'm going to be Clara in *The Nutcracker*."

"Wow," Mom said.

The beige lady beamed at me. "That will be a wonderful experience. You'll remember it all your life."

"I know," I said. "I'm *very* excited."

Mom handed the beige lady her shopping bag.

The lady thanked Mom and headed for the door. As she was walking out, O-tosan and Conrad came in.

"Maeve," O-tosan called. "Can we talk?"

"Okay," Mom replied. (Maeve is her first name.)

Just then the bushy-haired woman came up to us. "Do you have any dinner plates?" she asked my mother.

"Would you help this nice lady?" Mom asked me.

"Sure," I said.

The woman with bushy hair wanted to see practically everything in the store. While I was helping her, my mother slipped into the studio. I was almost positive I could hear my parents whispering.

When the bushy-haired woman finally left (without buying anything), the shop was empty. That wouldn't last long. I rushed into the studio.

The studio has several pottery wheels, two kilns (that's a powerful oven for baking pottery), and several big worktables. O-tosan and Mom were sitting at one of the tables, talking in low voices.

I glanced over at Conrad, who was wedging clay.

He shrugged.

"Please don't make me give up the part," I said.

"Your father and I are going to meet with Ms. Rosen on Tuesday," Mom told me.

"We want to ask her what she thinks about you being Clara," O-tosan explained. "If she says it's fine, then fine. If she says it will take too much time away from your schoolwork, then you'll have to give it up."

"Okay," I agreed. I wasn't happy, but at least I had a chance to keep the part.

"Is your prince cute?" Conrad asked.

"He's okay," I said.

"Do you like him?" Conrad asked, making a goofy face.

"Mom!" I yelled. "Make Conrad stop."

Mom ignored my outburst. "Madame Trikilnova called this morning," she said. "She reminded me that the Russian dancers are arriving on Monday."

"There's no way I could forget that," I said.

"Well, I hope you two won't fight while we have company," Mom said.

Conrad wrinkled his nose. "We'll see."

"We'll try not to," I promised.

Six

Something Wonderful

My first rehearsal for *The Nutcracker* was on Monday after school. My parents hadn't met with Ms. Rosen yet, so they let me go.

Pat was waiting for me in Studio C. She was teaching all the kids their parts.

Madame Trikilnova was going to work with the grown-ups. They were arriving from Russia later that afternoon.

"Have a seat," Pat said.

I plopped down in the center of the studio.

Pat sat on the floor, facing me. I felt strange, in a nice way, being all alone with my ballet teacher.

"Before we start, do you have any questions?" Pat asked.

"Yes." I took a deep breath. "Why did Madame Trikilnova pick me to be Clara?"

"Well," Pat said, "only Madame Trikilnova can

answer that. But I think she saw something wonderful in you."

"Something wonderful?" I asked.

"Sure," Pat said. "You're a good dancer. And you work harder than anyone else in your class. You'll make a great Clara."

"Thanks," I said.

"How do you feel about getting the part?" Pat asked.

"Excited," I said. "And nervous."

"I know," Pat said. "I was Clara when I was your age."

"You were?" I asked.

Pat nodded. "That's exactly how I felt, too. The best way to stop being nervous is to know your part really well. You were an angel last year, weren't you?"

"Yes," I said.

"Then you must know *The Nutcracker* pretty well," Pat said.

"I do," I said. "I saw it about a thousand times during rehearsals last year."

"Okay," Pat said. "Do you remember the part when the mice chase Clara?"

I nodded.

"What does Clara do?" Pat asked.

"Runs away," I said.

"Right," Pat said. "Today I'm going to teach you how to run."

"I know how to run!" I exclaimed.

"But you don't know how to run *onstage,*" Pat said. "You have to run fast without making any noise. It's not easy."

Pat and I got to work. She was right. Running the right way was difficult. Doing a bunch of fancy turns would have been easier.

After rehearsal I ran out to meet my family in front of the ballet school. It was time for the Russians to arrive!

My parents were talking to Jillian and her mother, Ms. Bell. Conrad was sitting on the curb, reading a comic book. Charlotte and her parents were there, too.

Jillian ran up to me. "How was your rehearsal?"

"Fun," I said.

"What did Pat teach you?" Jillian asked.

I giggled. "How to run."

Charlotte overheard what I said. She put her nose in the air. She probably thought Pat wouldn't have to teach *her* how to run.

A few seconds later Madame Trikilnova drove up. She parked, and the Russian dancers climbed out of her car. Two of them, a man and a blond woman, smiled at us. The third dancer was a dark-haired woman. Her eyes were red, and she was looking at her feet.

"Hello, everyone!" Madame Trikilnova sounded much more cheerful than usual. "I want you to meet our guests."

Madame Trikilnova put her arm around the sad-looking woman's shoulders. "This is Anna. She will be dancing the Sugarplum Fairy."

Anna looked up and smiled weakly.

"This is Galina, our Dewdrop Fairy," Madame Trikilnova said, indicating the blond woman. "And this is Yuri, who will be the Sugarplum Fairy's *cavalier.*" *Cavalier* is a fancy French term for a ballerina's partner.

Galina and Yuri flashed us smiles.

Madame Trikilnova started explaining something to the visitors in Russian.

"It looks like Anna's been crying," Jillian whispered.

I nodded. "I wonder what's wrong."

Madame Trikilnova turned to Ms. Bell. "Anna will stay with you, okay?"

"Of course," Ms. Bell said.

"Oh, great," Jillian whispered.

"Don't worry," I said. "I'm sure she'll cheer up."

Ms. Bell picked up Anna's bag. Anna, Jillian, and her mother said good-bye to everyone.

"Wish me luck," Jillian whispered.

"Good luck," I said.

Ms. Bell, Jillian, and Anna headed off toward the Bells' house. It's only a few blocks from Main Street.

"Mr. and Mrs. Stype," Madame Trikilnova said. "Galina will stay with you."

Mr. Stype had brought his fancy car to Main

Street. He opened the door for Galina.

"This is beautiful automobile," Galina said, choosing her words carefully.

"Thanks," Charlotte said smugly.

"Does everyone in America have nice automobiles?" Galina asked.

"Well, no," Mr. Stype sputtered. "We are very fortunate."

Galina misunderstood. "You are very *famous*? You are American rock star perhaps?"

"Of course not!" Mrs. Stype said.

Charlotte was staring at her guest as if she were a bug. Poor Galina!

Meanwhile, Mom approached Yuri. She held out her hand.

"My name is Maeve," she said slowly.

"Hello!" Yuri shouted, pumping her hand up and down.

Yuri had long dark hair and bright blue eyes. He was wearing a leather jacket and a fur hat. He must have been hot. The rest of us were wearing sweatshirts or light jackets. It never really gets that cold in Glory, even in December.

"Does he speak English?" I whispered to Madame Trikilnova.

Yuri heard me. "Of course!"

"A little," Madame Trikilnova added.

I swallowed a giggle. Yuri was proud of his English. But Madame Trikilnova didn't seem impressed.

"We will go out to dinner," O-tosan said.

Yuri looked puzzled.

Madame Trikilnova explained to him in Russian.

"Thank you," Yuri said.

I knew O-tosan was hoping to take our guest out for fish. Salmon is a specialty of Washington state.

We put Yuri's bag in the trunk of our car.

"What would you like to eat?" Mom asked Yuri slowly.

"American hamburger," Yuri answered immediately. "McDonald's!"

Mom and O-tosan traded looks.

Conrad looked up from his comic book for the first time. "All right!"

Seven

Russian Houseguests

On Tuesday Pat had me practice running again. At the end of the rehearsal, she gave me a big smile. "Good work!"

"Thanks," I said, beaming. Learning how to run had been hard, but not *that* hard.

When I got home, I turned on Tchaikovsky's Fourth Symphony and plopped down on my bed. Tchaikovsky is one of my favorite composers. He wrote the music for *The Nutcracker*.

I tried to relax. But I kept thinking about my parents. They were at school, meeting with Ms. Rosen. What was she saying? Would she tell my parents I shouldn't be Clara?

Someone knocked on my door.

"Come in!" I yelled.

Yuri poked his head in. "What are you doing?"

I sat up. "Listening to some music."

"But this is Tchaikovsky," Yuri said. "He is Russian. And he plays classic."

I laughed. "You mean *classical* music."

Yuri came into my room. "Where is your rock and roll? Rock and roll is American music."

"I listen to rock too," I said. "But I love classical music."

Yuri looked surprised.

"Most of my friends *don't* like classical music," I added quickly. "In fact, they think I'm pretty weird."

Yuri shook his head. "You are not weird. All good dancers love good music. Perhaps this is why you will be Clara."

"Maybe," I said. I liked that explanation.

"May I stay?" Yuri asked. "And listen?"

"Sure," I said.

Yuri sat down in my big armchair. He put his head back and closed his eyes. He was smiling.

I lay back and listened, too. But before the symphony was over, I heard the front door open. My parents were home! I jumped up and ran into the kitchen. Yuri didn't move.

Out in the kitchen, O-tosan was pouring two glasses of cranberry juice. Mom was looking through the newspaper.

"What did Ms. Rosen say?" I asked. "Do I still get to be Clara?"

"Sit down," Mom suggested. "We'll tell you all about it."

I pulled out a chair. “Well?”

Mom and O-tosan sat down, too.

“You can still be Clara,” O-tosan announced. “Ms. Rosen says playing the part will be good for you.”

“All right!” I exclaimed. “What else did she say?”

“Well, she said you’re very smart,” Mom said.

“Really?” I was surprised. If Ms. Rosen thought I was smart, why did she give me a *D* in spelling?

“She also said you should be getting better grades,” O-tosan said.

“I’ve been *trying,*” I said.

“That’s just what Ms. Rosen said,” Mom told me. “She says you’re one of her hardest workers. She doesn’t think it’s your fault you aren’t doing better.”

“She doesn’t?” I was getting confused. If it wasn’t my fault, whose fault was it?

“Ms. Rosen wants you to take some tests,” O-tosan said.

“What kind of tests?” I asked.

“Ones that will help explain why you aren’t doing better,” Mom said.

“What did you tell her?” I asked.

“We said it was okay,” Mom said. “What else would we say?”

I was already on my feet. “Mom!” I howled. “How could you do this to me? Why didn’t you ask me how I felt?”

“I don’t understand,” Mom said. “Why wouldn’t

you want to take the tests? They're going to help you."

"The other kids will think I'm some kind of freak," I said.

"That's not true," O-tosan said.

"Yes, it is," I insisted.

"Megan," Mom said. "I think you're overreacting."

"You're wrong!" I yelled.

All I could think of was a girl I had known in first grade. Suzie Simons. She had to go to a special class because she lisped. The other kids never let her forget it. They teased her so much, Suzie's parents finally moved her to another school. What if that happened to me?

"When do I have to take these tests?" I asked.

"Ms. Rosen said the sooner the better," O-tosan said.

"What does that mean?" I asked.

"The day after tomorrow," O-tosan said.

Great.

"You look worried," Becky told me Thursday at lunch. Becky, Megan, Nikki, and I were sitting at our usual table in the lunchroom.

Becky was right. I was worried. I had been ever since my parents told me about the tests.

"What's the matter?" Nikki asked.

I hadn't told my friends anything about the tests. I was hoping it would turn out that I was perfectly normal. Then my friends would never have to know anything about it.

"Nothing is the matter," I lied. I decided to change the subject before the others asked any more questions. "Did I tell you about Yuri?"

"What about Yuri?" Jillian asked.

"He's not an easy houseguest," I said. "Mom and O-tosan are fed up with him."

Becky took a sip of her juice. "What does he do?"

"He's a bathroom hog," I explained. "I don't know what he does in there, but it takes him hours."

"Is he still a McDonald's freak?" Nikki asked.

I nodded. "He loves all kinds of junk food. But his favorite is chocolate bars. He eats about twenty a day."

"He'd better watch out," Jillian said. "Madame Trikilnova will get angry if he gets fat."

"I don't think Yuri knows junk food makes you fat," I told her. "He thinks all Americans live on Coke and potato chips and chocolate. Conrad and Yuri get along great. They like to pig out together."

"Do you like Yuri?" Becky asked.

I nodded. "He's not easy to live with, but he's really nice. And he loves classical music, just like me."

"He doesn't sound as bad as Anna," Jillian said.

"What does she do?" Becky asked.

"Spends hours on the phone," Jillian explained. "One second she's laughing, and the next second she's crying."

"What does she say?" I asked.

"We don't know," Jillian told me. "She always speaks in Russian."

"Who's she talking to?" Becky asked.

Jillian shook her head. "We don't know. She hardly ever talks to us. She doesn't know much English. Unless Madame Trikilnova or one of the other dancers comes over, Anna stays in her room."

Just then the loudspeaker crackled. "Will Megan Isozaki please come to the nurse's office? Megan Isozaki, to the nurse's office."

My friends looked surprised.

I stood up and started to pick up my garbage. My hands were trembling.

"Why does the nurse want you?" Becky asked.

"Maybe I'm sick and I don't know it," I joked.

Ha, ha.

Eight

Too Many Tests

"Hi," I said as I walked into the nurse's office.

"Hi, Megan," the nurse replied.

The nurse's name is Lois. We got to know each other last year when Mark Miller—this gross boy in my class—knocked me down on the playground. I scraped up both of my hands. Lois cleaned my hands and gave me three Band-Aids. She's nice.

Lois was sitting next to the cot. A little boy—maybe a first-grader—was lying on it.

"I don't feel good," the boy told me.

"We know," Lois said, smoothing back his hair. "Your daddy is on his way."

"I hope you feel better soon," I added.

Lois winked at me. "Ms. Chadick is waiting for you in the next room." She pointed at a door.

I knocked on it.

"Come in!"

I opened the door.

Inside, an African-American woman was sitting at a desk. She stood up when I came in. She was wearing a red suit with a short skirt.

"Hi, Megan. I'm Ms. Chadick."

"Hi," I said shyly.

Ms. Chadick shook hands with me and told me to sit down. "First I'm going to ask you a few questions," Ms. Chadick said as she took her seat. "Then I'll give you some tests."

"Is this going to take a long time?" I asked.

"A while," Ms. Chadick said.

"Because I need to get back to class," I said.

"Does your teacher have something special planned?" Ms. Chadick asked.

"No," I said. "I just don't want my friends to worry about me."

"I see," Ms. Chadick said. "Well, I promise to go as fast as I can. What's your favorite subject in school?"

"Music," I said.

"Any others?"

"No."

"What's your favorite thing to do outside of school?" Ms. Chadick asked.

"Dance," I said. "I take ballet twice a week."

"That sounds like fun," Ms. Chadick said. While we talked, she took notes on a pad.

"Okay, here's the first test." Ms. Chadick handed me a paper and pencil. She took out a stack of cards.

"Each of these cards has a design on it. I'm going to show them to you one at a time. I want you to draw the designs."

I picked up the pencil.

"Do you always write with your left hand?" Ms. Chadick asked.

"Um, yeah," I said.

Ms. Chadick made another note on her pad. It was starting to bug me that she kept writing stuff down.

"Let's begin." Ms. Chadick showed me the first card. I tried to copy the design, but it was hard. I'm not good at drawing. After about twelve cards, Ms. Chadick said we had done enough. She put the cards away and gave me a new piece of paper.

"Now I want you to draw as many of the designs as you can from memory," Ms. Chadick said.

"No fair," I exclaimed. "Why didn't you tell me before?"

"Sorry," Ms. Chadick said. "Those are the rules."

I didn't like Ms. Chadick much. I drew as many of the designs as I could. I got about nine.

"Okay," Ms. Chadick said. "That's the end of that test."

"Can I go now?" I asked eagerly.

"Not yet," Ms. Chadick said. "I'm going to ask you some questions about the world. Some of the questions are for kids much older than you, so

don't be upset if you don't know all the answers."

I nodded.

"How many pennies are there in a nickel?" Ms. Chadick asked.

"Five."

"How many days in a week?" Ms. Chadick asked.

"Seven," I said.

"Name the days of the week in order," Ms. Chadick said.

"Sunday, Monday . . ." I said slowly. "Um, I always get the next one confused. Is it Thursday?"

Ms. Chadick shook her head.

"Then it's Tuesday," I said quickly. "Wednesday, Thursday, Friday, Saturday."

Ms. Chadick made a mark on her pad. "Good!"

We did the months next. I knew most of them. Then Ms. Chadick asked me the alphabet. I didn't do too well. I know there are twenty-six letters, but I get the order confused.

Ms. Chadick gave me a bunch more tests. After a while I stopped being nervous. I just wanted to get back to my class.

"Well, Megan," Ms. Chadick said when we finally finished. "You have a learning disability."

"What's that?" I asked. "I thought a disability meant, like, being blind. Or having to use a wheelchair."

"Those are kinds of disabilities, too," Ms. Chadick said. "Think of it this way. People use wheelchairs because it's hard for them to walk. Your disability makes it hard for you to read and to see numbers properly. That makes it difficult for you to learn the same way other children do."

"You mean I have a problem with my eyes?" I asked.

"No," Ms. Chadick said. "Your parents told Ms. Rosen that you had your eyes checked a few months ago. They're fine. Your problem is that the information your eyes see gets scrambled up before it gets to your brain."

"Are you sure?" I asked. "Maybe I'm just dumb."

Ms. Chadick smiled. "You're not dumb. You just need to go about learning in a different way."

"How did I catch this disability?" I asked.

Ms. Chadick shook her head. "You didn't catch it. People are born with learning disabilities."

"Can I get rid of it?" I asked.

"No," Ms. Chadick said. "But I can teach you how to work around it."

Ms. Chadick gave me lots of papers to give my parents. "We're going to be meeting twice a week," she told me.

"What for?" I asked.

"We're going to work on your reading and your math," Ms. Chadick said. "We'll listen to books on tape. And I'll bring in a computer for you to work on. We'll have a good time."

Ms. Chadick was trying to make having a learning disability sound like fun. But I knew she just wanted to cheer me up. I didn't feel cheery. Who ever heard of a Clara with a learning disability?

Nine

Two Awful Classes

"What did the nurse want?" Nikki asked me later that afternoon.

Nikki, Jillian, and I were walking to ballet. (Becky hardly ever waits for us. She likes to get to class early. We're too slow for her.)

"Um, she gave me a test," I said.

"Like, an eye exam?" Jillian asked.

"Kind of," I said.

"So, is everything okay?" Nikki asked.

"Sure," I lied.

My friends started talking about what they wanted for Christmas. I wasn't listening. I was wondering how my brain was scrambling things up. *Maybe trees don't really look like that,* I told myself. *Maybe the sidewalk is different, too.* I had lived in Glory all my life, but that afternoon it seemed unfamiliar.

We walked by Mr. Byrne and Mr. Frantz. They're

these two ancient men who always sit on a bench in front of the bank.

Mr. Frantz tipped his hat. "Afternoon, girls."

Mr. Byrne pulled something out of his inside jacket pocket. "Looky here, Megan," he called. "We got our *Nutcracker* tickets. We can't wait to see you on opening night!"

"Thanks," I replied. But my stomach did a nervous flop. I wasn't sure I wanted to be Clara anymore. I was afraid my learning disability would make me mess up.

I walked into Studio C a few minutes later. I felt as if everyone was looking at me. Charlotte was definitely staring. "How's my Clara today?" Pat greeted me.

"Fine," I mumbled.

Pat started the barre with the usual *pliés*.

The barre is the part of ballet class I do best. But that day my body felt stiff and clumsy.

Pat watched my *pliés* and frowned. "This is our last class together until after *The Nutcracker*," she said. "I want you guys to have some fun today. Loosen up. Enjoy it."

I knew Pat was talking to me. And I tried to have fun, I really did. But I felt as if I had never done the exercises before. It was like a part inside my head had snapped.

We moved into the center. Charlotte and Lynn stood just in front of me.

"I can't believe Madame Trikilnova made *her* Clara," Charlotte whispered. "She can't even dance."

"She can so," Lynn whispered.

"Maybe Madame Trikilnova felt sorry for her," Charlotte whispered.

I should have been mad, but I wasn't really. Maybe Charlotte was right. Why else would Madame Trikilnova let a girl with a learning disability be Clara?

"Okay, kids," Pat called. "Let's end with a combination." This is what we were supposed to do:

Start with a *sous-sus.* (That's a kind of quick *relevé.*) Travel forward with a *pas de bourrée.* (A *pas de bourrée* is three tiny, crossed steps.) Do a *développé* forward with our right legs. (That means we had to slowly stretch our right legs out to the front.) *Tombé* (or "fall") forward into another *pas de bourrée.* Then finish with a *changement* (a small jump), ending with the right foot in front.

"Let's dance together," Jillian suggested.

"All three of us," Becky added.

"How come?" I asked. Usually, Becky and Jillian like to go in one of the first groups. I always go in the last.

"We want to dance with you," Jillian explained.

"Well, okay," I agreed.

Becky, Jillian, and I watched the other kids dance. They did the combination without too much trouble.

Jillian, Becky, and I stepped forward last.

Everyone was watching. Charlotte was staring right at me.

Al began to play.

The three of us did the *sous-sus* and the *pas de bourrée*. Then my mind went blank. I couldn't remember what was next. Becky and Jillian kept dancing. I should have followed their movements, but I didn't. I just froze.

Charlotte giggled.

Becky and Jillian finished.

Jillian turned to me. "Are you okay?"

"Should we do it again?" Becky asked Pat.

Pat glanced at me. "No. I think that's enough for today."

Becky looked surprised. Pat usually likes us to do things until we get them right. I wondered why she hadn't made me do the combination again. I decided she felt sorry for me, too.

"Megan Isozaki, please report to the nurse's office," came a voice over the loudspeaker the next afternoon.

Jillian shot me a puzzled look.

"Do you have to take another test?" Becky whispered.

"I don't know," I lied.

When I got to the nurse's office, Lois wasn't around. But Ms. Chadick was in her room. She looked cheerful, which made me feel grumpy.

"Sit down," Ms. Chadick suggested.

"I don't want to," I told her.

"Okay," Ms. Chadick agreed. "It's fine if you stand."

I flopped down in a chair.

Ms. Chadick smiled. "I always start my classes the same way. You get to tell me one good thing and one bad thing that happened to you since the last time I saw you."

"Nothing good has happened," I said. "I'll tell you two bad things instead."

"That's fine," Ms. Chadick said.

"I gave my parents the papers you gave me," I started. "They read them and decided my brother should get tested, too. Conrad is mad, and he thinks it's all my fault. Well, he's wrong—it's your fault!"

"What was the other bad thing?" Ms. Chadick asked quietly.

"Ballet!" I hollered. "I was going to be Clara in *The Nutcracker*. I was going to be a star. But people with learning disabilities can't dance! How can you dance when everything in your brain is scrambled?"

"Megan—"

"No!" Hot tears sprang up in my eyes. "You lied to me. You said you were going to make things better. But you didn't. You ruined everything!"

I ran out of the office, down the hall, and into the rest room. I locked myself in a stall.

Ms. Chadick followed me. "Megan, please come out."

"No," I said. My tears were slowing down. I felt calmer. But I still didn't want to talk to Ms. Chadick.

"I'm going to leave you alone," Ms. Chadick said. "But, believe me, things are going to be fine."

After she was gone, I came out. I washed my face and went back to class. I got there just in time for a spelling test.

Jillian and Becky were busy numbering their papers. They didn't notice I had been crying.

I sat down and took the test.

Ms. Rosen graded it.

I got a *D*.

Ten

Juicy

"Hi!" Dean said later that afternoon. He was standing in the hallway outside Studio C. He was dressed in black tights, a white T-shirt, and black slippers.

Dean and I were about to have our first rehearsal together.

"Hi," I said. I was too upset to be excited to see Dean. I was worried about rehearsal. What if I messed up? Dean would never like a girl with a learning disability.

"Um, why aren't you inside?" I asked.

Dean shrugged. "Door's locked."

"Did you knock?" I asked.

"No," Dean said. "Do you think someone is inside?"

"Could be," I said.

Dean knocked.

About one second later Pat opened the door. "Hi, kids," she said. "Is it three thirty already?"

"It's three thirty-five," Dean said.

Pat moved out of the doorway. "Well, then, let's get to work."

I wasn't surprised Pat had locked the door. See, she broke her ankle last year. She had just started to dance again. She likes to practice alone. I followed Dean into the studio—and then I *was* surprised. Guess who was in there? Yuri!

"Hello, Megan," Yuri said.

"Ah, hi," I said.

"Yuri, this is Dean Stellar, our prince," Pat said.

"I've heard much about you," Yuri said.

"You have?" Dean asked.

I squeezed my eyes closed. Yuri had heard of Dean because Conrad had been teasing me about him all week. What was he going to say?

"Yes," Yuri said. "You are a big star in Glory."

"I am?" Dean asked.

"Yes," Yuri said. "I was drinking Coke in the coffee shop on Main Street this morning. My waitress spoke of you."

Dean laughed. "That's because she's my mother! She's always bragging about me."

Mr. and Mrs. Stellar, the twins' parents, own the coffee shop on Main Street. The whole town hangs out there, especially kids from the ballet school.

"My mother brags about me, too," Yuri said. He turned to Pat. "Thanks for dancing with me."

"My pleasure," Pat said.

"Good-bye," Yuri said. And then he was gone.

Pat was all smiles.

"Do you like him?" I asked. What I meant was, Do you like him as a boyfriend?

"I sure do," Pat said.

Wow! I couldn't wait to tell my friends. This was juicy!

"Okay, guys," Pat said. "I want to work on a section of the ballet near the end of Act One. I'm going to pretend to be the Mouse King and chase you, Megan."

"All right," I agreed.

Pat pulled the chair away from the piano. "This will be your bed. When I chase you, you are going to run to the bed. Once you get there, pretend to faint."

It was much harder than Pat made it sound. I had to get to the bed in a certain number of steps. And, once I got there, I had to fall into the bed in just the right way. Pat and I tried it a million times before I got it right.

Dean got bored. "When do I get to do something?"

"I was just getting to that," Pat said. "Megan, once you faint, lie still. That's when you, Dean, get to stab the Mouse King."

"All right!" Dean said.

It was my turn to get bored. I sat in the chair and watched while Dean and Pat practiced. It took at least fifteen minutes before Dean stabbed Pat the right way.

"What's next?" I asked. I had come to rehearsal expecting a nightmare. But so far it had gone fine. I had even picked up an interesting piece of gossip.

"You should still be lying still," Pat told me.

I flopped back on the chair and closed my eyes.

"Now, Dean, you walk over to Megan," Pat said. "Count your steps: one, two, three, four. When you get to the bed, pick up Megan's hand and kiss it . . ."

I didn't hear the rest of what Pat said. I couldn't believe what I had already heard. Dean had to kiss me? This was terrible! How could I have forgotten that the prince kissed Clara?

"Okay, guys, let's try it from the top," Pat suggested.

We took our places. Pat chased me. I ran and pretended to faint onto the bed. Dean pretended to stab Pat. I had my eyes closed, but I could hear Dean walking toward me. One step. Two. Three. Four. Dean reached for my hand, and—I pulled it away.

I opened my eyes.

Dean and I giggled.

Pat smiled and shook her head. "Come on, kids. There's no reason to feel funny about the kiss. Remember, you're *acting*. Now, let's try it again."

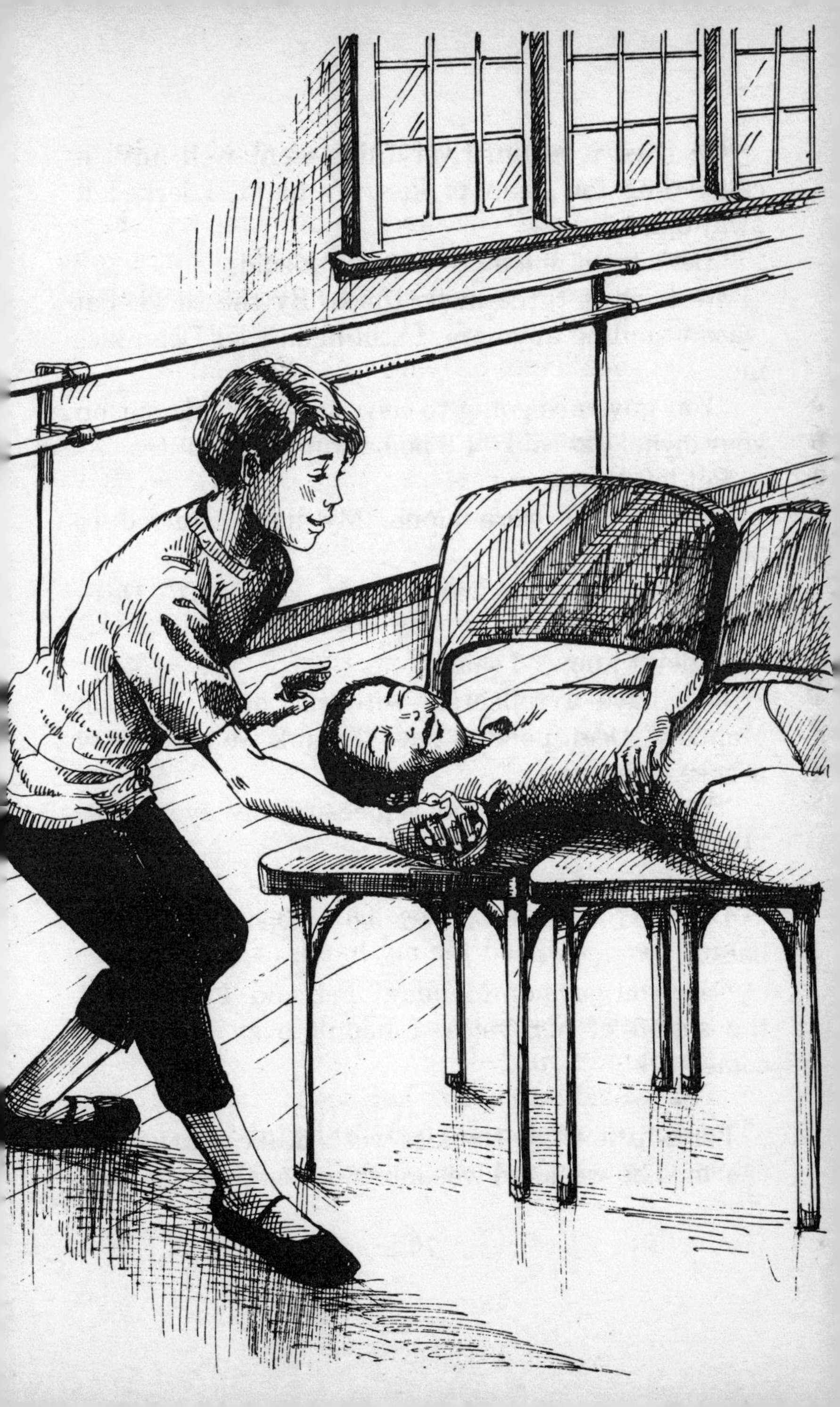

We tried it again. Everything went well until it came time for Dean to kiss my hand. I jerked it away again.

"Let's try it one more time," Pat said.

We tried it three more times. By the third, Pat wasn't smiling anymore. I still hadn't let Dean kiss me.

"You guys are going to have to work this out on your own," Pat said. "I'll be back in ten minutes."

Pat left the studio.

Dean and I were alone. My heart started to pound.

"Why don't you want me to kiss you?" Dean asked.

"I don't know," I said.

"We have a rehearsal with the other kids on Monday," Dean pointed out. "I think we should try it once before then."

"You're right," I said, squeezing my eyes shut. "Do it."

Dean kissed my hand. It felt . . . nice.

I opened my eyes and smiled at Dean. He smiled back.

"See you guys on Monday," Pat said. I jumped at the sound of her voice. I hadn't even heard her come back.

For a little while the kiss worked like a good-luck charm. The weekend was much better than the past few days had been. Conrad wasn't mad at me anymore. There weren't any tests to take or special classes to attend. Still, I was worried about being Clara. And once Monday rolled around and rehearsals began again, my good-luck charm wore off. . . .

Eleven

Kissing in Public

"I saw them together!" Jillian squealed on Monday. She had just burst into the dressing room at the theater.

"Really?" Nikki said.

"Where?" Katie asked.

"What were they doing?" Becky asked.

Ever since I had seen Pat and Yuri together, my friends and I had been spying on them. Katie had seen them talking in Madame Trikilnova's office on Saturday morning.

I pulled on my leotard. "Hurry up and tell us. Rehearsal is about to begin. Madame Trikilnova will freak if we're late."

Madame Trikilnova was getting nervous. We had only two weeks to rehearse before opening night. The ballet had to be perfect by then. Once we opened, there wouldn't be time to fix anything. We would perform once every day for a week—right up to Christmas Eve.

To me, opening night still seemed a long way away. I was more worried about the kiss.

"I just saw them in the coffee shop," Jillian reported as she dressed. "Yuri was drinking a Coke. He had his hand on Pat's arm, and she was laughing."

"Wow," I said.

"How romantic," Becky said.

"Yeah, this is great," Risa said. "Pat hasn't had a boyfriend for as long as I've known her. And that's been more than a *year*. I don't want her to end up an old maid."

"She's not old!" Katie exclaimed.

"Old enough," Risa said.

The dressing room door opened, and Charlotte came in.

Nikki made a face. "Come on, let's go."

My friends and I walked out into the theater. It was crowded. Almost all of the kids in the cast were there.

Some men were stacking pieces of the set in the wings of the stage.

Al was practicing *Nutcracker* music on the piano. He made a few mistakes, but the music was still beautiful.

Katie came up behind me. "There's Dean. He looks cute today."

"Katie—" I said.

"Cute enough to kiss," Nikki added.

"Megan's not going to kiss him," Katie said. "Dean's going to kiss *her*."

I groaned. "Don't remind me."

"You might as well admit—" Katie started.

"I don't like Dean," I interrupted.

Pat climbed up on the stage and clapped her hands. "We need to get started, so listen up! Your costumes are here. Everyone has to go to their dressing room to try them on. When you're finished, come right back to the stage. We have a lot of work to do!"

"I hope this takes a long time," I whispered to Jillian as we stood in line.

"How come?" she asked.

"So we don't have time to get to the kiss," I explained.

But the mothers who were in charge of costumes were organized. The line moved quickly. Soon I was trying on my two costumes. They both fit perfectly.

I was going to wear a party dress in the first few scenes. Then I would change into a white nightgown, white tights, and white slippers for the rest of the ballet. In Act II, I also got to wear a veil and a crown.

My costumes weren't fancy. But they were magical. Once I slipped that nightgown over my head, I almost believed I could be Clara.

About forty-five minutes later everyone was back onstage. Pat asked us to do Act I from the battle to the end. It was the part of the ballet that included the kiss.

The soldiers and mice had their big battle. The battle continued until the Mouse King challenged Dean to a duel. After the duel, Pat announced, "This is when Clara hits the Mouse King with her slipper. We'll practice that part at our next rehearsal. We'll skip it for now."

From then on it was the part Pat, Dean, and I had been practicing on Friday. Pat, who was still pretending to be the Mouse King, chased me to the bed. I fainted. Dean stabbed Pat. And then Dean was walking toward me. One step. Two. Three. Four.

Even with my eyes closed, I could feel everyone watching. At the last second I snatched my hand away.

Pat groaned.

The other kids giggled.

"Aw, go ahead and kiss him," John Stein called.

I opened my eyes.

"Megan!" Dean looked furious. "We practiced this!"

The other kids thought that was pretty funny.

"I bet you guys practice *all the time,*" one of the guys called.

Even my friends laughed.

I jumped up. "I'm telling all of you once and for all. I don't like Dean. I—I hate him!"

Dean's face turned bright red. He opened and closed his mouth, but no sound came out.

I slapped my hand over my mouth. Why had I said that? It wasn't true.

Dean ran off the stage.

"Come back!" Pat called.

"Should I go after him?" Becky asked.

Pat sighed. "Yes."

Becky ran out into the hallway. I studied the floor. I was too embarrassed to look at the other kids.

My friends came over to me.

"Are you okay?"

"Don't worry."

"You can tell Dean you're sorry at school."

Becky came back.

"Did you find him?" Pat asked.

"No," Becky said.

"That's all for today," Pat said. "I'll see you all tomorrow."

The other kids started to leave. They were whispering about what had happened. I had ruined rehearsal. And I was going to ruin the whole ballet. I just knew it.

Twelve

Slipper Blues

Brrring!

"There's the bell," Becky said Tuesday morning before school. "We'd better line up."

I looked around the playground. "Dean and Philip still aren't here."

"They'll be here," Jillian said. "Dean wouldn't skip school just because he's mad at you."

The three of us got in line. Ms. Rosen started to lead our class into the building.

"You think he's still mad at me?" I asked.

Jillian twisted a lock of hair. "Well—"

"I think so," Becky admitted. "You broke his heart yesterday."

"That's silly," I said. "Dean's not in love with me."

Jillian and Becky traded glances.

"He's not!" I insisted.

"Here he comes," Becky whispered.

Dean and Philip ran to join the end of the line.

They were tossing a football back and forth.

"I'm going to talk to him," I said. I stepped out of line and let the other kids flow past me. When the twins caught up, I hurried along beside them.

"What do you want?" Philip asked in a nasty voice.

I pretended not to hear Philip. "Hi, Dean."

"Hi," Dean replied. He stopped walking.

I stopped, too. I thought Dean wanted to talk. But he called, "Hey, Phil, go out for a pass!"

Philip ran down the hallway. Dean whizzed the football to him. Philip grabbed it and pulled it into his chest.

"Great catch!" Dean yelled. He ran to meet his brother, leaving me all alone. My chest ached. I knew I had really hurt Dean's feelings.

Rehearsal that afternoon was terrible. Everyone was curious about my fight with Dean. They were staring at me. I hoped no one could tell I had a learning disability just by looking.

"We're going to practice the scene where Clara hits the Mouse King with her slipper," Pat announced. "Everyone but Megan can have a seat on the stage. But please don't leave. I'm going to need the rest of you soon."

Jillian grinned at me. "Have fun."

"Thanks," I said.

"The Mouse King will be standing right here—

next to the Christmas tree." Pat made a big gesture with her arm.

We all giggled. The Christmas tree wasn't actually there yet.

In some productions of *The Nutcracker,* a little tree grows to an enormous size in the middle of Act I. We couldn't do that in our tiny theater. We were going to have a real live tree instead. I thought that was just as special.

Pat walked across the stage. "You'll be standing here, Megan."

I stood in the place Pat was pointing to.

Pat moved back into the Mouse King's position. Yuri was going to play the Mouse King during performances. But I wouldn't get to practice with him until dress rehearsal.

"Try to hit me in the middle of my back," Pat called.

I glanced around the stage. Becky and Jillian were watching me. Nikki was braiding Risa's hair. Katie was reading a book. Most of the mice and soldiers and angels looked bored.

Dean was sitting next to Charlotte. I was surprised by that. I didn't think Dean liked Charlotte any more than I did.

"Go ahead," Pat called. "I'm ready."

I bent my arm back and threw. The slipper landed about a foot in front of me.

Dean and Philip laughed.

Hillary Widmer jumped up. She's a Blue who is in my class at school. Hillary picked up the slipper and handed it to me. "Throw it sooner," Hillary whispered.

I took the slipper and nodded. Hillary is a terrific softball player. I figured her advice would really help me.

Pat turned her back to me.

I squinted at her, bent my arm back, and threw. This time the slipper flew to the left and landed in the orchestra pit.

Philip climbed down to get it.

"Thanks," I said as he handed me the slipper.

"Do you know what your problem is?" Philip asked.

I thought Philip was going to give me advice, like Hillary had. "No, what?"

"You throw like a girl," Philip said loudly.

Several kids giggled.

I grabbed the slipper from Philip. I threw it without thinking. The slipper hit my foot.

The other kids howled.

"It's not funny!" I burst out.

"Not all girls throw like that," Charlotte announced. "I have great aim."

Dean laughed. "Too bad you're not playing Clara."

Tears sprang to my eyes. I almost wished Charlotte *was* playing Clara. Then I wouldn't have to ruin the ballet. But I didn't want Dean to want

Charlotte to be Clara. It meant he liked her better than me.

Pat made me work on my aim for a long time. It didn't get any better. I wasn't surprised. I probably couldn't throw for the same reason I got *D*s in school. My brain was broken.

The rest of the cast grew restless.

Finally Pat gave up on me. "Let's run through the battle scene," she suggested.

"But what if I can't hit the Mouse King?" I asked.

"Don't worry," Pat replied. "You still have a while to practice. Try to work on your aim at home."

"Okay," I whispered.

The mice and the soldiers were in the middle of the battle scene when Madame Trikilnova rushed into rehearsal.

Madame Trikilnova whispered something to Jillian. Then she hurried over to Pat and whispered something to her.

"I'm sorry, kids," Pat called. "We're going to have to quit early. I'll see you tomorrow."

Pat and Madame Trikilnova rushed out of the theater.

"What did Madame Trikilnova tell you?" I asked Jillian. The other kids gathered around, too.

"She said Anna's going back to Russia to get married," Jillian reported. "Her flight leaves this afternoon."

"Who's going to be our Sugarplum Fairy?" Becky asked.

"Beats me," Jillian said.

I looked around the stage. My friends looked disappointed. Not me. I had to bite back a smile. I could have turned a hundred *pirouettes*. I didn't have to be Clara. *Yippee!*

"Madame Trikilnova will have to cancel the performance now," I said, trying to sound sad.

"No she won't," Dean said. "She'll just find someone else to dance the Sugarplum Fairy."

"Like who?" I asked.

"Just someone," Becky said.

"Well, I don't know," I said. "It took her months to get Yuri and Galina and Anna here."

Katie patted my arm. "Don't worry. We wouldn't let Madame Trikilnova cancel *The Nutcracker*. You're going to be Clara."

I sure hoped Katie was wrong.

Thirteen

Upside Down and Backward

That night I had a nightmare. . . .

I walked onstage wearing the pretty white nightgown Clara wears.

The theater was full. Mom, O-tosan, and Conrad were in the audience. My grandparents from Ireland and my grandparents from Japan were there, too. So were all of my aunts and uncles and cousins. Ms. Rosen and Ms. Chadick were sitting together. Pat's Pinks were there. So were Nilas Martins and Darci Kistler, two famous dancers.

Dean and Charlotte were sitting in the front row. They were holding hands and laughing.

They were laughing because I was messing everything up. I was a learning-disabled dancer. I went left instead of right. I did a *plié* instead of a *relevé*.

I took off my slipper and threw it. It hit Dean

in the face. He put his hand up to his nose. When he took his hand away, it was covered with blood.

I woke up, my heart racing. The ballet was going to be a disaster. I had to get out of being Clara before it was too late.

"I have to talk to you," I whispered to Nikki Wednesday at lunch.

"Okay," Nikki said. "But let's sit down first. I'm starving." She motioned toward the table where our friends were already sitting.

"No," I said. "I have to talk to you alone. Come on, let's get into the lunch line. I want Becky and Jillian to think we're buying cookies."

Nikki followed me into line, just like I knew she would. Nikki is a curious person. She can never resist hearing secrets.

"What's up?" Nikki whispered.

I glanced around. Two sixth-grade girls were in line in front of us. The kids behind us looked older too.

"I don't want to be Clara," I whispered. "You have to help me get out of it." Nikki is good at coming up with sneaky plans. That's why I asked her for help instead of Jillian.

"Is this because of Dean?" Nikki asked.

"That's one of the reasons," I said.

"What are the other ones?" Nikki asked.

"None of your business!" Sometimes Nikki is too curious.

Nikki shrugged. "I thought you wanted my help." She started to get out of line.

"Fine," I said, pulling Nikki back in front of me. "I'll tell you. I don't think I'm good enough to be Clara. I think I'm going to mess up."

"Is that all?" Nikki asked. "Listen, don't worry. You just have stage fright. You'll get over it."

"Nikki," I hissed. "I have a learning disability. I can't dance the part. You saw how I messed up yesterday at rehearsal. I *can't* do it."

We had reached the desserts. Nikki took a plate of peanut-butter cookies. So did I.

"When did you get this learning disability?" Nikki asked.

"I've always had it," I told her. "But I just found out about it last week. Listen, if you won't help me, I'll figure it out myself."

"No," Nikki said quickly. "I'll help you."

We had reached the end of the line. "That will be seventy cents," the cashier said.

Nikki looked at me.

"What?" I asked.

"I don't have any money," Nikki explained.

I groaned and handed the cashier a dollar.

Nikki took a bite of one of her cookies while I waited for my change. "I need some time to think. I'll call you after dinner, okay?"

I nodded. “One more thing. When I drop out, Becky will get my part. I don’t want her to feel guilty. So promise me that you won’t tell her anything about this.”

Nikki crossed her heart. “Promise.”

Fourteen

An Award-Winning Performance

"Madame Trikilnova is still trying to find a new Sugarplum Fairy," Katie told us that afternoon at rehearsal. Katie knows about everything that goes on at the ballet school. She earns her ballet lessons by helping Madame Trikilnova. On the days she works in the office, she spies.

"What's she doing?" I asked.

"Spending a lot of time on the phone," Katie reported. "And scribbling on a yellow pad."

"Has she found anyone?" Becky asked.

Katie shook her head. "And she's *not* in a good mood."

We didn't need Katie to tell us that. Ever since Anna had dropped out, Madame Trikilnova had been walking around with an enormous frown on her face.

When Nikki called me later that night, my mom was sitting right next to me. We couldn't make secret plans with her listening in. We decided to talk the next evening.

Things were quiet at school on Thursday. Ms. Chadick was out for the entire week. I didn't have to worry about being called out of class until Monday.

In rehearsal on Thursday afternoon, we worked on Act II. Clara hardly does anything in that act. It's full of grown-up solos. Dean still wasn't speaking to me. I was miserable.

After dinner that night, I sneaked into the kitchen and called Nikki while Yuri and my family were decorating the house for Christmas. "Did you think of a way I can get out of dancing Clara?" I asked.

"Play sick on opening night," Nikki suggested.

"No," I said. "I have to drop out as soon as possible."

"How come?" Nikki asked.

"Because of Becky," I said. "If I drop out on opening night, she won't have any time to rehearse."

"Good point," Nikki agreed. "Well, we could give you a serious illness. Do you think you could play sick for a week?"

"No," I said. "But I won't have to. All I have to do is miss one rehearsal. Once Pat and Madame Trikilnova see Becky onstage, they'll want her to be Clara."

"I really don't think so," Nikki said. "She's not that much better than you are."

"Trust me," I said.

"If you say so," Nikki said. "But if Becky gets to be Clara, I hope you get another part."

I didn't tell Nikki, but I didn't want another part. Ballet was too hard for a person with a learning disability. I didn't think I was even going to take lessons again in the spring.

On Friday my friends and I went to the coffee shop after rehearsal.

"Madame Trikilnova still hasn't found a Sugarplum Fairy," Katie announced.

"Do you think *The Nutcracker* will be canceled?" I asked.

"No way," Katie replied. "Madame Trikilnova says the ballet will go on even if she has to dance the Sugarplum Fairy herself."

I was glad I had my secret plan.

A run-through of Act II was scheduled for Saturday. The entire cast was coming, even the grown-ups.

"Better hurry," Mom said when she came into my bedroom Saturday morning. "It's getting late. Yuri is dressed and ready to go. He's in the kitchen right now, drowning his pancakes in syrup. You shouldn't keep him waiting."

I sat up with a soft groan. I swallowed, pretending that it really hurt. "Okay, Mom," I said weakly. "I'm getting up."

“Do you feel okay?” Mom asked.

“Sure,” I said. “My stomach just feels a little funny.”

“Well, then, don’t get up yet,” Mom said. “I want to take your temperature.” She went to get the thermometer from the bathroom.

As soon as Mom was gone, I leaped out of bed and did jumping jacks. When I heard her footsteps coming down the hall, I popped back under the covers.

Mom sat down next to me. She put her hand on my forehead. “You feel hot,” she reported. “And you look flushed.”

Of course I was hot and flushed. My heart was beating a million miles an hour. Jumping jacks will do that to you.

Mom stuck the thermometer in my mouth. I yanked it out and jumped out of bed.

“Stomach,” I yelled, running for the bathroom.

“Do you want me?” Mom called.

“No!” I ran into the bathroom, carefully leaving the door open a crack. I had left a tall glass of water on the back of the toilet. I poured it into the bowl. It made a splash that sounded just like someone throwing up.

I flushed, heated the thermometer near the lightbulb, stuck it back into my mouth, and walked slowly back to bed.

Mom looked worried. She had smoothed out my

covers while I was gone. I crawled into bed.

Mom tucked me in and checked the thermometer. "You've got a fever," she announced.

"I don't care," I said. "I want to go to rehearsal. I *have* to go."

"Sorry," Mom said. "But I think you'd better stay in bed." Mom went off to tell Yuri to leave without me. She also called Madame Trikilnova. They were on the phone for a long time. I felt sorry for Madame Trikilnova. First she lost her Sugar-plum Fairy—and now me. But I reminded myself that I had a terrific understudy. I imagined how happy Becky would be when she found out she could be Clara.

Mother and O-tosan came into my room.

"I'm going to stay home from work," Mom told me. "I'll be right downstairs in case you need anything."

"You don't need to stay home, Mom," I said. "It's almost Christmas. The shop will be super busy."

"You're more important," O-tosan told me.

"I'll be fine," I said. "I can call you if I need you."

O-tosan and Mom were both shaking their heads.

Conrad appeared in my doorway. "How about if I stay home and watch Megan?"

"I don't know . . ." Mom said.

"We'll be fine." Conrad led Mom and O-tosan away from my door. "You can trust me."

A few minutes later my parents were gone.

Conrad poked his head into my room. "You're faking, right?"

I nodded. "Thanks for getting them to leave."

"No problem," Conrad said. "My band's coming over in ten minutes. We needed a place to rehearse. This is it."

Fifteen

That's My Part!

My brother's band is called Acid Rain. They're always looking for a place to rehearse. That's because nobody can stand to listen to them.

Conrad plays lead guitar, and he's not that bad. The band's big problem is Paul, the singer. His voice cracks all the time, and I think he's tone-deaf. The other members of Acid Rain don't seem to mind. "Our music isn't pretty," Conrad says. "But neither is life." I wonder what Paul would think if he knew Conrad listened to opera every night before bed.

After Conrad left my room, I got dressed in a hurry. I didn't want to be in my pajamas when a bunch of teenage boys got to my house. I shouldn't have worried. When the band arrived, they headed right for the basement. (They like dark places.) Pretty soon, squeaks and wails drifted upstairs.

I turned on my stereo and put on my headphones. I couldn't hear Acid Rain anymore, but I could *feel* them. The noise coming from downstairs was so loud, it made my bed tremble.

I started to wish I was at the theater. Not dancing. Just watching. I wanted to see Madame Trikilnova's face when she realized how good Becky was. But, of course, I couldn't let Madame Trikilnova—or anyone—see me.

That's when I remembered the balcony. Conrad is always bragging about it. See, a few years ago, Conrad discovered a door in the back of Glory theater. Beneath the door was a welcome mat. Under the mat was a key to the door.

The door led to the balcony of the theater. A long time ago you must have been able to walk from the first floor of the theater up to the balcony. But those passages had been closed up.

Sometimes Conrad and his friends watch movies for free from the balcony. My friends and I tried it once. But the balcony gave us the creeps. Besides, we felt bad about sneaking in without paying. We hadn't been up there in a long time.

Well, that was about to change.

I ran all the way to the theater. The key was under the mat, just like it was supposed to be. I opened the door and sneaked up to the theater's balcony. Nobody saw me.

From the balcony, I had a perfect view of the stage. A lot was going on!

The stage had been turned into the Land of

Sweets. The set showed a forest, and a castle made of gingerbread and gumdrops.

The orchestra pit was filling in. Al was at the piano, of course. A teenage girl with braces was plucking the harp. Mr. Stellar was playing the oboe. (O-tosan had to miss rehearsal to be at the shop.)

My eyes drifted to the stage, and I made an amazing discovery. Madame Trikilnova had found a new Sugarplum Fairy: Pat!

Pat and Yuri began to dance their *pas de deux*, the most beautiful part of the entire ballet. Pat was up on pointe. (That means she was dancing on her toes.)

Yuri tenderly held Pat's wrists as she went into a perfect *arabesque penchée*. She bent over at the waist, with her right leg extended so far up, her toes pointed at the ceiling.

Later Yuri lifted Pat right up off the ground. In his arms, she held her arms back and pointed her toes. Her head was near the ground. It looked as if she were making a graceful dive.

I hardly breathed until the *pas de deux* was over. I felt so proud of Pat. I looked around the stage for my friends. I knew they must be freaking. That's when I realized . . .

Becky wasn't there.

Charlotte was playing Clara!

Sixteen

Tennis Shoes in Bed

I sneaked out of the balcony just before the rehearsal ended. Charlotte looked so smug, I started to feel sick for real. I wished I had a rotten tomato to throw at her.

Where was Becky?

A few minutes after I got home, someone knocked on my bedroom door. I dove into bed, put my head down on my pillow, and tried to look sick.

"Come in," I called.

Yuri poked his head into my room. "You weren't feeling well this morning. Your mother told me. How you feel now?"

"Okay," I said. "Come in."

Yuri came in and sat down in my big armchair.

"How was rehearsal?" I asked.

"Awful," Yuri said. He pulled a chocolate bar out of his jacket pocket and started to unwrap it.

"Did Madame Trikilnova find a new Sugarplum

Fairy?" I asked. Of course, I already knew the answer. I just didn't want Yuri to know I knew.

"Yes," Yuri said. "The answer was right on her nose."

I giggled. "You mean, right *in front of* her nose."

"Yes," Yuri said. "Thank you for correcting me. Madame Trikilnova has chosen Pat to dance the Sugarplum Fairy."

"Pat!" I was still playing dumb. "That is so great."

"Yes," Yuri agreed. "She is wonderful."

Wow! What a romantic thing to say.

"We really missed you," Yuri said.

"Didn't Becky do a good job?" I asked.

"Not there!" Yuri announced.

I pretended to be surprised. "She wasn't there? Then who played Clara?"

"That little monster Galina stays with," Yuri said.

"Her name is Charlotte," I told him.

"That Charlotte thinks she is a princess," Yuri said. "She expects everyone to start clapping just because she doesn't fall off her seat."

I didn't even laugh at what Yuri had said. I was too angry.

"That's just like Charlotte!" I exclaimed, sitting up straighter. I didn't want Yuri to see I was dressed, so I pulled up my covers. But I pulled them up too far. My feet stuck out at the bottom. I still had my shoes on.

Yuri stared at my shoes. "You're not truly sick, are you?"

"No," I admitted. "I'm just pretending. Please don't tell Mom or O-tosan."

"I won't," Yuri promised. "But why are you pretending this?"

"Um . . ." I didn't want to tell Yuri about Dean or my learning disability. "Do you know the part of the ballet where Clara hits the Mouse King with her slipper?"

Yuri nodded.

"I have terrible aim," I said. "I can't hit *anything* with a slipper."

Yuri frowned at me. "Don't all Americans play baseball?"

I smiled. "No."

"Well, I do," Yuri said. "I will teach you how. Then you will be Clara, and we will get rid of the monster."

Yuri popped the last of his candy into his mouth and stood up. "We will go to the park immediately."

How could I say no? Yuri knew I wasn't sick. And I had plenty of time. Mom and O-tosan wouldn't be home for hours.

"Let's go," I said, climbing out of bed.

"We will need a ball," Yuri said.

"We have one," I said. "I'll get it."

I was going with Yuri to practice my aim. But I hadn't changed my mind about being Clara. I still didn't think I could do it without messing up.

Seventeen

Just on the Cheek

"Put 'er here," Yuri yelled a little while later. He pounded his fist into O-tosan's softball mitt. He looked like a real major-league baseball player. He was even chewing gum.

I examined the ball. It was a softball. (We didn't own a real baseball.) Nobody had used it in years. Its seams were bursting.

"Come on!" Yuri yelled.

I bent my arm back and threw. The ball landed right in front of my feet—just like the slipper had in rehearsal.

"You must let go sooner," Yuri told me. That's what Hillary had said, too.

I picked up the ball and tried again. This time I didn't hold on so long. The ball landed closer to Yuri. But not much.

"Do again," Yuri called. "But do not bring your arm so far back."

I picked up the ball and tried again. And again. And again.

Softball might be an American game, but Yuri knew a lot about it. He gave me advice, and my aim slowly improved. After about twenty minutes I actually hit his glove.

"All right!" Yuri called.

"I can't believe it!" I yelled. I was surprised. I thought I couldn't throw because of my learning disability.

Yuri tossed me the ball. "Do again."

"Okay," I agreed eagerly.

It took a few tries, but I hit the glove again. "Did you see that? It was perfect!"

Yuri didn't answer. He was looking at something behind me. I turned around.

Dean was walking down the sidewalk. His hands were shoved into his pockets. He was looking at his shoes.

"Hello, prince!" Yuri yelled. "Want to play ball?"

Dean turned toward us. "Oh, hi!" He pretended to be surprised, but I knew he had already seen us.

"Want to play ball?" Yuri repeated.

"Uh, I guess." Dean walked up to me. "I thought you were sick."

"I was," I replied. "Well, sort of. Anyway, I feel fine now."

Yuri came over and handed Dean the mitt. "You catch, I'll watch."

At first, throwing the ball to Dean made me nervous. My aim got worse. Yuri had to call out a lot of advice. Once I started to relax, my aim improved. Dean relaxed, too. He stopped looking so mad.

"I need a Coke," Yuri suddenly announced. He headed toward the coffee shop.

Dean tossed the softball in the air. "Do you want to practice some more?"

"No." I walked over to a swing and sat down. "Um, Dean? I—I'm sorry about what happened at rehearsal the other day." Dean sat down on the other swing. He stared at his feet.

"Don't worry about it. You were probably just embarrassed or something."

"Yeah," I said. "I was."

Dean looked up at me and grinned. "I can't wait until rehearsal tomorrow. Everyone will freak out when they see how well you throw now."

I pushed myself back and forth with one foot. "I won't be at rehearsal tomorrow."

"Why not?" Dean asked.

"I'm not going to be Clara," I told him.

"But you only missed one rehearsal," Dean said. "Madame Trikilnova won't be mad."

"It's not that." My throat felt pinched together. "I just don't want to mess everything up."

"Don't worry," Dean said. He twisted his swing so that he was facing me. "I know a trick to cure stage fright."

"Well, that's only part of the problem. . . ." I couldn't meet his eyes.

"Just try it, okay?" Dean went on. "Tell me your favorite part of ballet."

"You don't understand," I started.

"Come on," Dean urged. "Tell me."

"The music, I guess."

Dean looked surprised. "Okay," he said, shrugging. "If your favorite part is the music, you should focus on the music. You'll forget to be scared."

"Dean," I whispered. "I have a learning disability."

Dean gave me a funny look. "Really?"

"Yes," I said. "And so there are some things I just can't do. Like dance."

"That's not true," Dean said.

"It is so!" I yelled. "You don't know anything about it!"

"Yes, I do!" Dean yelled. Then he took a deep breath. "My older cousin has a learning disability. He told me all about it. Lots of famous people have them."

"Like who?" I asked.

"Steven Spielberg," Dean said. "He's a famous movie director. He made *ET* and *Jurassic Park*."

"I know who Steven Spielberg is!" I yelled. "I have a learning disability, but I'm not stupid!"

"I didn't say you were," Dean said. "I just wanted to tell you that my cousin says—"

"I don't care what your cousin says!" I yelled. "I'm sure he doesn't know anything about dancing!"

Dean got a funny look on his face. "Actually, he does. He dances with the New York City Ballet."

"Really?"

Dean nodded.

"Someone with a learning disability dances for the New York City Ballet?" I asked.

"Why not?" Dean asked. "*You* have a learning disability, and you're a good dancer."

"Do you really think so?" I asked.

"You're a much better Clara than Charlotte," Dean said. "She's a pain."

I was so happy that, without thinking, I leaned over and kissed Dean on the cheek. Poor Dean turned bright red.

"I'm sorry—" I started. But before I could say anything more, Dean kissed me back. On the lips!

Eighteen

Dress Rehearsal

"How are you feeling?" Mom asked when she and O-tosan got home that evening.

For a second I didn't know what she meant. I had forgotten that I was supposed to be sick. "Much better," I finally said. "What's for dinner?"

Mom and O-tosan traded smiles.

"Spaghetti," Mom said. "But not for you. Since you were sick to your stomach this morning, you'd better stick with dry toast tonight."

"Dry toast?" I repeated. "But I'm starving."

"Then I'll make you some chicken broth too," O-tosan said.

When we all sat down to eat, I was nervous. Conrad and Yuri both knew I had been faking that morning. I was afraid they might give me away. But they didn't. They were too busy gobbling up huge platefuls of pasta.

After dinner I called Nikki. I told her I had seen the rehearsal from the balcony.

"Wasn't Pat great?" Nikki asked.

"Yes," I said. "But where was Becky?"

"She's really sick," Nikki reported. "Katie went over to her house, but Mrs. Hill wouldn't let her in. Whatever she has, it's catching."

I sighed. "Do you think she'll still be sick on opening night?"

"Probably," Nikki said. "She's not even allowed to come to the phone."

"Wow," I said. "Well, listen, if Becky is sick, I'm going to be Clara. We can't let Charlotte get it."

"Great!" Nikki sounded really happy.

I took a deep breath. I wasn't sure how happy *I* was.

Mom called Madame Trikilnova later that evening and told her I was feeling better. Just like that, I had my part back.

I got to the theater around nine o'clock the next morning. Madame Trikilnova had scheduled a dress rehearsal. Act I in the morning. Act II in the afternoon.

The theater was buzzing with activity.

Jillian and Nikki were hanging out in the hallway outside the dressing room.

"You look great," I told them.

Jillian was wearing a green velvet dress with a white lace collar. Her hair was down, and she was wearing a big white bow in it.

Nikki made a face. "I look great for a *boy*." She

was dressed in bright-yellow knickers and an orange top.

"You'd better get into the dressing room," Jillian said. "It takes a long time to get dressed."

"Okay," I agreed. "See you guys later."

I pushed open the door to the girls' dressing room. The scene inside was crazy. Girls were crowded around the mirrors, fussing with their hair. Older girls were helping younger ones zip up their dresses and straighten out their tights. Everyone was talking and laughing at once.

Katie's mom, Mrs. Ruiz, was helping an angel fix her wings. I hadn't seen Mrs. Ruiz in a few months. Her belly was getting really big. Mrs. Ruiz was expecting a baby in a couple of months. Katie was getting super excited.

Mrs. Norg, Nikki's mom, was surrounded by tubes of pancake makeup, eyebrow pencils, lipstick, and who-knows-what-else. She was putting the finishing touches on someone's makeup. Wait! Not just *someone*—

"Becky!" I called, hurrying over to her.

Mrs. Norg was smoothing lipstick on Becky's lips. Becky turned to look at me.

"Keep your head still!" Mrs. Norg barked.

Becky jerked her head back.

"What are you doing here?" I asked Becky. "I thought you were sick."

Becky waited until Mrs. Norg finished her lipstick.

Then she pulled me aside. "I was just pretending to be sick," she whispered.

"Why?" I asked.

Becky took a deep breath. "Promise not to be mad?"

"I guess," I said.

"Nikki told me *you* weren't really sick," Becky said. "We wanted you to come back. We figured the best way to do that was to let Charlotte have your part."

I tried to be mad. "Nikki *promised* me she wouldn't tell."

"Don't be mad," Becky said. "She was trying to help."

I smiled. "I'm not mad. It's nice to be back."

Charlotte stomped by us. She was carrying her mouse head. She did not look happy.

I felt like being naughty. "Thanks for filling in for me yesterday," I called after her.

Charlotte spun around to face me. "It wasn't just for yesterday."

"What do you mean?" Becky asked.

"Madame Trikilnova won't be very happy when she finds out you two skipped rehearsal yesterday," Charlotte said.

My hands started to sweat. How did Charlotte know about that?

"We were sick," Becky said.

"For one day?" Charlotte asked.

"It was the twenty-four-hour flu," Becky said.

Charlotte pointed her finger at me. "Then how come I saw you playing ball in the park yesterday afternoon?"

"You saw me?" I repeated. Why hadn't I been more careful?

"So maybe it was a twelve-hour flu," Becky said.

Charlotte smirked. "Just wait until Madame Trikilnova finds out. I bet she throws you both out of the ballet."

Just then Madame Trikilnova pushed the door open. Pieces of hair were falling out of her usually perfect bun. She was carrying a clipboard full of messy papers.

"I want the party children onstage!" Madame Trikilnova called. Then she caught sight of me. "Miss Isozaki, why aren't you dressed?"

"Sorry," I yelped. I hurried toward the rack of costumes.

Becky grabbed my arm. "Makeup first. Come on. I'll help you."

Charlotte walked up to Madame Trikilnova. "I want to tell you something."

"Not now." Madame Trikilnova clapped her hands. "Places, everyone!"

"But it's *important,*" Charlotte whined.

Madame Trikilnova sighed. "Very well. What is it?"

Charlotte motioned for Madame Trikilnova to

come closer. She whispered in her ear. Madame Trikilnova glanced over to where Becky was putting makeup on my face.

"Miss Isozaki! Miss Hill!" Madame Trikilnova hollered. "I want to speak to you in the hallway immediately."

Becky put down the makeup. Her hand was shaking. I tried to swallow, but I couldn't get my throat to work.

Madame Trikilnova marched out into the hallway. Becky and I followed.

"Have fun," Charlotte called after us.

"Miss Isozaki," Madame Trikilnova said. "Miss Stype just told me you weren't really sick yesterday."

My throat felt like it was covered with dust. "I—"

"Being Clara is a big responsibility," Madame Trikilnova said. "Part of that responsibility is to come to every rehearsal. Now, if you don't want the part, just tell me."

I didn't say anything. My mind was spinning. I had been trying to get out of being Clara almost since I got the part. Now all I had to do was say I didn't want it, and the part would be Becky's.

"Megan just has stage fright," Becky said.

"If you don't want the part, Miss Hill can take over," Madame Trikilnova told me.

"No!" Becky said. "Megan wants the part."

"I'd like to hear that from her," Madame Trikilnova said.

"I want to be Clara!" I burst out. "I'm sorry I missed rehearsal. But I definitely want to be Clara."

Madame Trikilnova's face softened. "That's good. Don't worry about your stage fright. Everyone gets it. Now, hurry up and get dressed. Everyone is waiting for you."

Becky and I hurried back into the dressing room. Charlotte was standing near the costume rack. All of the party children had already gone into the wings.

"You're still a mouse," Becky told Charlotte.

"More like a rat," I said.

Charlotte looked so disappointed, I almost felt sorry for her. *Almost.*

When we got out onstage, Madame Trikilnova told us we were going to run through the entire ballet. If we made a mistake, we had to keep going.

Act I began. There were a few problems.

Tad—the kid who was playing Fritz—was supposed to *pretend* to break the nutcracker doll. Tad gave the doll such a whack, it broke for real.

Jillian leaned against part of the set, and it fell over. But when I threw my slipper, it hit the Mouse King right in the head! A perfect shot! Yuri growled and chased me. He was much more frightening than Pat.

It was almost time for the kiss. As I waited with my eyes closed, I thought about Dean. I realized my friends had been right all along. Dean really seemed to like me. There must be something pretty special about me, after all.

When Dean kissed my hand, I didn't feel at all embarrassed. I felt tingly and happy. It was nice.

My friends were allowed to go home at lunchtime. None of them were in Act II.

"Madame Trikilnova says we can stay if we're quiet," Jillian told me.

"Are you going to?" I asked.

"Sure," Jillian said. "We want to see Pat and Yuri dance together."

It was worth waiting for. Pat and Yuri were perfect. You could tell they were in love by the way they danced.

"It's so romantic," Becky said as we were leaving the theater late that afternoon.

"I think it's sad," Katie said. "What's going to happen when *The Nutcracker* ends? Yuri will have to go back to Russia. They're both going to be brokenhearted."

Becky sighed. "That's what makes it so romantic."

Nineteen

Vowels

The next morning the loudspeaker at school crackled. "Megan Isozaki, please report to the nurse's office," came a voice.

Becky and Jillian watched as I stood up. This time they didn't look worried. They looked jealous.

A few minutes earlier Ms. Rosen had written a list of words on the blackboard. We were supposed to put them all in a story. Some of the words—like "fundamental" and "scamper"—were nearly impossible to work in.

I knew my friends would eventually ask why I kept being called to the nurse's office. The question was, What would I tell them?

I walked down the hall. My palms were sweaty. I hadn't seen Ms. Chadick since my first awful class with her. Would she be mad at me?

"Hello, Megan," Ms. Chadick said when I walked into her room.

"Hi," I said.

Ms. Chadick patted the sofa next to her. I sat down.

"Remember the rules," Ms. Chadick said. "You get to tell me one good thing and one bad thing."

"Right . . ." I said. "Well, I learned how to throw a ball—which I thought I couldn't do because of my learning disability. Also, I found out that a boy I like likes me. And I decided to be Clara in *The Nutcracker,* after all."

"That was three good things!" Ms. Chadick looked impressed. "What about something bad?"

I thought for a second. "I got a *D* on my spelling test."

"Well, that's what we're here to work on," Ms. Chadick said.

We got down to work. Ms. Chadick said we were going to start with reading. And we were going to start at the very beginning. We did the alphabet. Then we talked about vowels. I practiced my spelling on a computer for a little while. Before long my hour with Ms. Chadick was over.

"I'll see you on opening night," Ms. Chadick said before I left.

"What do you mean?" I asked.

"I'll be in the audience," Ms. Chadick explained. "I always go to see my students perform."

That gave me a shiver. It was just like my dream. But I realized I wasn't worried about being a learning-disabled dancer anymore.

"I'm glad you're coming," I told Ms. Chadick. "*The Nutcracker* is going to be the best!"

When I got back to class, we were about to have a spelling test. I sat down and numbered my page. As Ms. Rosen called out the words, I remembered some of the things Ms. Chadick had taught me. I changed a few answers.

"Good work," Ms. Rosen said when she handed back my paper. I had gotten a *C*! It wasn't a great grade, but it was a big improvement.

"You guys?" I said to my friends after rehearsal that afternoon. "Let's go to the coffee shop. I have something important to tell you."

"Good idea," Katie said. "I'm starving."

"Me too," Becky agreed.

We started down the street.

Jillian fell in step next to me. "Is everything okay?"

I smiled. "Everything's fine."

We sat down in our favorite booth and emptied our pockets onto the table. Between the six of us, we had $3.96. We ordered french fries, onion rings, and a large Coke to share.

I cleared my throat.

Jillian was looking at me, waiting to hear what I had to say. But she was the only one.

Becky was trying to get the ketchup to come out

of the bottle. Risa and Nikki were signing their names over and over on a napkin. Katie was busy gobbling up the fries.

"I have something extremely important to tell you guys," I said. That got their attention.

"What?" Katie asked.

"I have a learning disability," I announced.

Nikki looked disappointed. "Is that all? You already told me about that."

"Katie, don't eat all the fries!" Risa said.

"I'm not," Katie said. "Don't get so hyper."

"Will you have to change schools?" Jillian asked.

"No," I said. "But I have to go to a special class twice a week."

"Is that why you keep getting called to the nurse's office?" Becky said.

I nodded.

Jillian took a sip of Coke. "What time is your class?"

"It's always different," I said.

"Maybe you can make it so you miss gym." Jillian and I both hate our gym teacher. She blows her whistle in our faces.

"What are you doing?" I asked Risa and Nikki.

Risa giggled. "Practicing our signatures. Just in case anyone asks for our autographs on Saturday."

"You guys don't seem very concerned about my learning disability," I said irritably.

"Well, what can't you do because of it?" Risa asked.

I thought for a minute. "I can do anything. But some things—like reading and math and spelling—are harder for me."

"So, what's the big deal?" Katie asked.

I shrugged.

"What do you guys think I should get my mom for Christmas?" Becky asked.

I listened to my friends discuss their Christmas shopping. I was amazed they weren't more upset about my learning disability. What was wrong with them? I had really expected them to be upset. I figured they just didn't think it was anything to be upset about. Maybe they were right.

"Pass the onion rings," I said.

Twenty

Curtain Call

I woke up very early on Saturday. That night was opening night!

I was jumpy. I couldn't watch TV or wrap Christmas presents or do homework. Finally I locked myself in my room and listened to *The Nutcracker* three times. I pictured where I would be onstage at each point in the music. Even though I'd been hearing the music for weeks in rehearsal, I wasn't sick of it.

My parents came home from the shop at around five o'clock. "Megan!" O-tosan called from downstairs. "We have to leave soon. Come eat!"

I hurried downstairs. "Please don't make me eat. I have butterflies in my stomach."

"Just try," Mom said. "I don't want you fainting onstage."

I sat down at the table. Conrad and Yuri were already there.

Yuri made a face as O-tosan dished out home-made vegetable soup. "This looks like something we'd eat in Russia."

"It's nutritious," O-tosan said. "For a dancer, you don't have very good eating habits."

Yuri waited until O-tosan turned back to the stove. Then he took a bite of his soup and made an awful face.

I giggled.

The phone rang.

"Eat," Mom ordered. "I'll get it."

Mom was back a minute later. "It's for you," she told Yuri.

Yuri picked up the phone in the kitchen. He babbled away in Russian long enough for his soup to get cold. He was grinning like mad the whole time.

"Who was that?" I asked when he hung up.

"Don't be so nosy," O-tosan told me.

"I don't mind," Yuri said. "It was my wife."

I almost dropped my spoon. Yuri was married! I couldn't believe it.

Poor Pat! There was no way she knew she was in love with a married man. I tried to figure out what to do. Should I talk to Yuri? Tell Pat? Mind my own business? I decided to ask my friends when I got to the theater. Jillian would know what to do.

Conrad brought me back from my daydream. "Why are you so quiet? Are you nervous?"

As soon as Conrad asked if I was nervous, I was. "A little," I admitted.

"Just try not to think about all of those people watching you," Conrad suggested. "It's only the entire town. I'm sure nobody will laugh if you mess up."

I put down my spoon.

"Are you okay?" Conrad asked. "You look green. Hey, wouldn't it be funny if Megan puked onstage?"

"Conrad!" O-tosan said. "Leave your sister alone."

"May I be excused?" I asked.

Mom nodded. "Go get your stuff together. It's almost time to go."

"Break a leg," Conrad said as I left the kitchen. "In fact, break two!"

O-tosan, Yuri, and I walked to the theater together. When we got there, people were already waiting outside.

Yuri winked at me. "Your fans are here."

I gulped.

Inside, Yuri hurried off to his dressing room.

"You'll be wonderful," O-tosan told me. He held up his flute case. "Just remember—you're not the only one who's nervous."

I laughed. "Don't worry. You'll be wonderful."

O-tosan headed for the orchestra pit. I made my way into the girls' dressing room.

Jillian and Nikki were standing near the mirror,

putting on lipstick. The rest of my friends hadn't arrived yet.

Mrs. Norg did my makeup. While I slipped on my costume, I told Nikki and Jillian about Yuri's wife.

"You're kidding!" Nikki said.

"Do you think Pat knows?" Jillian asked.

"No," I said. "Do you think we should tell her?"

"Yes," Jillian said. "But not now. News that bad could ruin her performance."

"You're right," Nikki agreed.

"Let's tell her at the party," I suggested.

"Okay," Jillian agreed.

Becky and Katie and Risa arrived. Jillian and Nikki told them about Yuri. I didn't join in the conversation. I was thinking about what I had to do in Act I.

"Megan?" Jillian asked. "Are you okay? You look funny."

I felt funny, too. "I'm scared."

"Take deep breaths," Jillian suggested. "That will calm you down." She took a few herself.

Mom came backstage. She was wearing a fancy black dress.

"You look pretty," I told her.

"Not as pretty as you," Mom said.

"Thanks," I said.

"Conrad and I have seats right up front," Mom told me.

Madame Trikilnova came into the dressing room. She was back to her usual tidy self.

"I'd better go," Mom whispered. She gave me a quick good-luck hug and left.

"Party children—five minutes," Madame Trikilnova called. Then she came over to me. "Miss Isozaki, it's time for you to be onstage."

I took a shaky breath. "Everything is happening so fast."

"You'll feel better once we get started," Madame Trikilnova said.

My friends wished me good luck. Then Madame Trikilnova led me onto the stage. Tad was already there. I sat in a chair behind the closed curtain. Tad sat on the floor next to me. As soon as the curtain went up, everyone would be able to see us.

"Break a leg," Madame Trikilnova called softly.

"Why did she say that?" Tad whispered. He usually has plump rosy cheeks, but he looked pale.

"It means good luck," I whispered.

"Oh . . ." Tad didn't say anything more.

I listened to the orchestra warming up. I could just make out O-tosan's flute.

My heart was beating a thousand miles an hour.

The audience was noisy. It sounded as if a thousand people were all talking at once. But a few seconds later everyone quieted down.

"We'd better close our eyes," I whispered to Tad. Clara and Fritz are asleep when *The Nutcracker* opens.

Tad closed his eyes and put his head on my

knees. The orchestra started to play the overture. I closed my eyes, too. And then I panicked. Why hadn't I given Becky my part? I didn't want to be Clara. I was much too scared.

I was supposed to count notes as the orchestra played. It was the only way I would know when to open my eyes. But I was so nervous, I lost count. I kept my eyes closed. If I opened them, I would see all those people staring at me.

"Now!" Madame Trikilnova whispered from the wings.

Tad poked me.

I didn't open my eyes. I heard the audience shifting in their seats. Madame Trikilnova was whispering with someone backstage.

Suddenly I remembered what Dean had said in the park: Focus on the music. I tried it. The orchestra finished the overture. There was a pause. Then they started the music over from the beginning. Without thinking, I started to count notes. When I got to the right number, I opened my eyes.

Know what? I couldn't see the audience, after all. The lights were too bright. But I could see the orchestra. O-tosan was there, playing his flute. The conductor gave me a nod.

I shook Tad awake. *The Nutcracker* had begun. What a relief!

The party guests started to arrive. I felt better once my friends were onstage with me.

Herr Drosselmeyer is a magical character in *The Nutcracker*. He's the spooky old man who gives Clara her nutcracker doll. Guess who played Herr Drosselmeyer? Madame Trikilnova! She wore a gray wig, and a patch over one eye. Mr. Stein had played Herr Drosselmeyer in rehearsals, so all of us kids were surprised to see Madame Trikilnova. She was good.

We did the Grandfather's Dance, which is a slow waltz. Then the party scene was over, and my friends left the stage.

In the next scene, I'm onstage all alone. I didn't feel as scared as I had in the beginning. All I had to do was pretend to go to sleep, holding the nutcracker doll.

The mice and soldiers came onstage and had their big battle. The Nutcracker and the Mouse King started to duel. It was time for my big throw. It didn't go well. I missed the Mouse King completely. I was disappointed, but the audience didn't seem to notice.

The Mouse King chased me back to my bed, I fainted, and Dean stabbed the King. Before I had time to worry about it, Dean kissed my hand.

A few minutes later Act I was over.

During the break between Acts, I told Madame Trikilnova I was sorry I messed up the beginning.

"Don't worry," Madame Trikilnova said. "You're doing a great job." That made me feel pretty good.

In Act II, Dean—oops, I mean my Nutcracker Prince—and I traveled to the Land of Sweets.

The Sugarplum Fairy greeted us.

Pat looked beautiful. She was wearing a short, stiff tutu. Sparkling silver wings were attached to her shoulders.

Then came Dean's big moment. He stood center stage and acted out the battle scene from Act I. The audience really clapped when he finished.

After that Dean and I sat on a throne and watched the dances that followed. Some are named after things to eat: Chocolate, Coffee, Tea, and Marzipan.

The Russian dance was one of my favorites. The dancers leap very high and do fast turns.

The Waltz of the Flowers was beautiful, too. Galina was the Dewdrop Fairy. She did an incredible *grand jeté*. (That's a spectacular kind of jump where your legs are in a split.)

Finally Pat and Yuri took center stage.

First Yuri danced a quick, flashy solo. Pat also danced alone. Then the two of them joined together for their *pas de deux*. They were terrific.

When the ballet was over, everyone got to take a curtain call. That's when you stand onstage while everyone claps for you. At first the entire cast was onstage. Then people started to leave in groups—the party children, the angels, the mice . . .

Finally just Dean, Fritz, and I were left with the

grown-ups. Then Fritz left. Then Dean.

I stepped forward all by myself. Conrad brought me up a bunch of roses. Then I ran offstage. All of my friends were waiting in the wings. We clapped for Galina, Pat, and Yuri.

After the curtain calls were over, Jillian gave me a hug.

"You were great," she said.

"Thanks!"

Lots of people came backstage and congratulated me. Mom took my picture. Mrs. Stellar said I was "stunning."

After I had talked to everyone, I took Jillian's hand and pulled her down the hall.

"Where are we going?" Jillian asked.

"You'll see!" I stopped in front of Pat and Galina's dressing room, and knocked.

Pat came to the door. "Good work tonight, girls," she greeted us.

"Thanks," we both said.

"Can we have your toe shoes?" I asked.

"Sure," Pat said. "Come in."

Ballerinas wear toe shoes to help support them while they dance on pointe. But toe shoes are fragile. If you have a big part with lots of jumps in it, you can only wear them once. Ballerinas go through a lot of toe shoes. It's expensive, but it's important to protect your feet.

Pat and Galina signed the shoes from that performance for us. Jillian and I each got one shoe from each of them.

"I'm going to hang mine on my wall," Jillian told me once we were back out in the hall.

"Me too," I agreed. "That way I'll always remember my first performance as Clara."

Later there was a party at the coffee shop. My whole family came. Almost the entire town of Glory was there.

Yuri and Conrad ate plate after plate of french fries.

"Did you tell Pat about Yuri yet?" Becky asked me.

"No, not yet," I said.

"We'd better tell her now," Jillian decided. "Where is she?"

I started to say "I don't know," but just then Pat walked in. And she wasn't alone. A cute guy was with her.

"Who's that?" I whispered to Jillian.

She grabbed my hand. "Let's go find out."

Jillian and I walked over to Pat. Before we could get a word out, Pat gave the strange man a long kiss.

When it was over, Pat noticed me and Jillian. We must have looked surprised, because Pat started to laugh.

"Who's he?" Jillian blurted out.

"This is my friend Luke from Seattle," Pat told us.

"Pleased to meet you!" Luke shook our hands.

"What about Yuri?" I asked.

"What do you mean?" Pat looked confused.

"We thought you—" I started.

"Aren't you in love with him?" Jillian asked.

Pat burst out laughing. "Yuri and I are just friends. What did you kids think?"

Luckily, someone tapped me on the shoulder just then. I turned away from Pat. Dean was standing behind me. "Hi," I said.

"Hi," Dean replied. He pulled a package out from behind his back. "I got this for you."

"Thanks," I said, surprised.

Dean and Jillian and I sat down at a booth.

I unwrapped my present. It was a brand-new softball.

"Whenever you want to practice your aim, call me," Dean said.

Jillian was smirking, but I didn't care.

"I love it," I told Dean. Then I leaned over and kissed my Nutcracker Prince right on the lips.

I've never seen Jillian look more surprised.

Arabesque Penchée

The Five Basic Positions

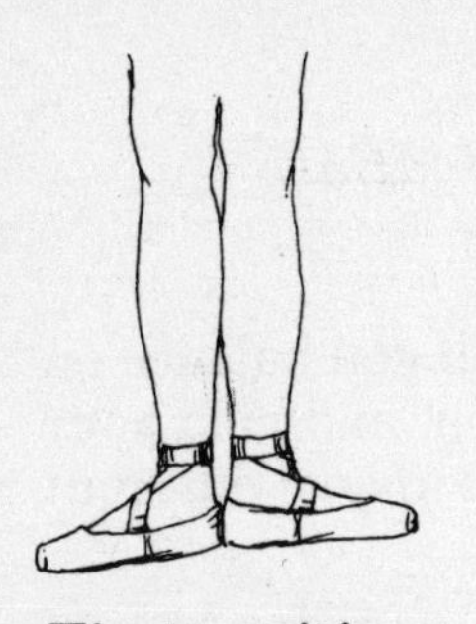

First position

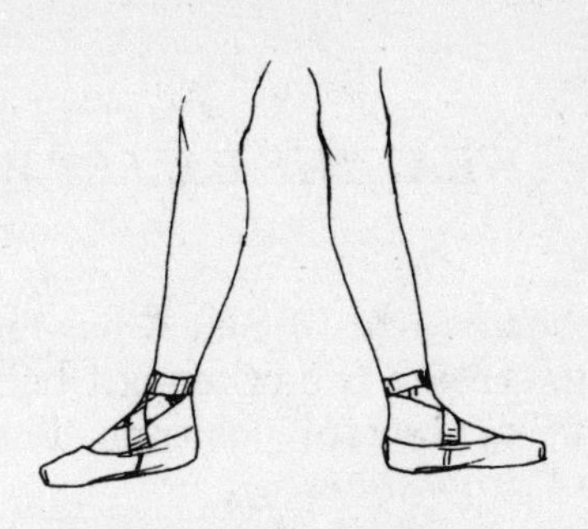

Second position

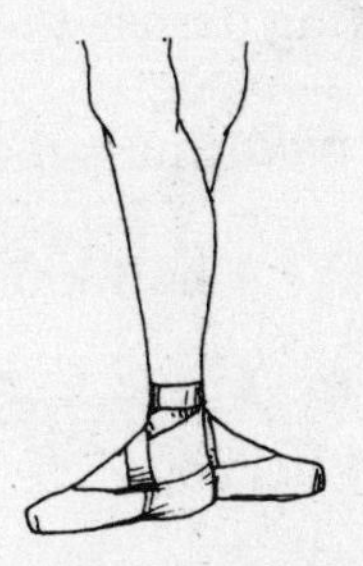

Third position

Fourth position

Fifth position

WHAT THE BALLET WORDS MEAN

Arabesque (a-ra-BESK) A pose in which you balance on one leg, stretch the other out behind you, and hold your arms in a graceful position. There are many different kinds of *arabesques*.

Bourrées (boo-RAYS) A series of tiny steps that make a dancer look as if she is gliding across the floor.

Cavalier (ca-va-LEER) A ballerina's male partner.

Demi-plié (de-MEE plee-AY) A half knee-bend.

Développés (dayv-law-PAY) An exercise in which the dancer slowly stretches out her leg.

Emboité (say ahn-bwah-TAY) A graceful jump in which you land with one foot in front of the ankle of the other foot. Also called a *petite jeté*.

Grand (gron) means "big" or "large" in French. A *grand plié* is bigger than a *plié*.

Jeté (je-TAY) A type of jump. In a *grand jeté* the dancer opens her arms and legs wide.

Pas de deux (pah duh duh) Dance for two, usually a man and a woman.

Pas de bourrée (pah duh boo-RAY) A traveling step.

Penché* or *Penchée (pahn-SHAY) Leaning. An *arabesque penchée* is a kind of *arabesque* in which you lean forward, lower your head, and lift your raised leg as high as you can.

Pirouette (peer-oo-ET) is French for "whirl." It's a kind of turn in which the dancer spins around on one foot.

Plié (plee-AY) is a knee bend. A *grand plié* is bigger than a *plié*.

Pointe Dancing on pointe means dancing on your toes. Ballet dancers use special shoes to dance on pointe. Girls start dancing on their toes when they are about twelve. Before then, their bones are too soft.

Positions Almost every step in ballet begins and ends with the dancer's feet in one of five positions. The positions are called first, second, third, fourth, and fifth. The drawing on p. 133 shows how the positions look. Some ballet instructors use French words to describe the positions: *première, seconde, troisième, quatrième,* and *cinquième.*

Relevé (ruhluh-VAY) An exercise in which you rise up on the balls of your feet.

Sous-sus (sew-SOO) A fast kind of *relevé*.

ABOUT THE AUTHOR

Emily Costello was born in Cincinnati, Ohio, and now lives in New York City. She likes to eat spaghetti, play tennis, and see movies. She has two left feet but enjoys watching ballet.

Also available in this series

1 Becky at the Barre

"I'm always going to remember this day," I announced. "Even when I'm a prima ballerina."

Becky is delighted to be moved up a class at ballet school. Her dancing is bound to improve and she can be with her friend, Katie!

But then Becky meets Charlotte, the best dancer in the pink class. It seems only natural to stand next to Charlotte to learn from her, and to go to her house to practise ballet.

She doesn't mean to leave Katie out, but soon the two girls argue. What can Becky do? How can she choose between her best friend and her new friend, between her best friend and ballet . . .?